# Plundered Range

Center Point
Large Print

Also by Will Ermine and available from
Center Point Large Print:

*Outlaw on Horseback*

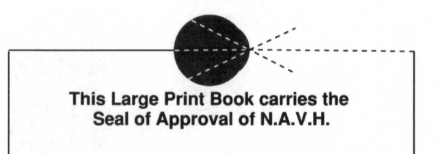

**This Large Print Book carries the
Seal of Approval of N.A.V.H.**

# Plundered Range

## WILL ERMINE

CENTER POINT LARGE PRINT
THORNDIKE, MAINE

This Center Point Large Print edition
is published in the year 2017 by arrangement with
Golden West Literary Agency.

First US edition: William Morrow & Company
First UK edition: Nicholson and Watson

The text of this Large Print edition is unabridged.
In other aspects, this book may vary
from the original edition.
Printed in the United States of America
on permanent paper.
Set in 16-point Times New Roman type.

ISBN: 978-1-68324-624-4 (hardcover)
ISBN: 978-1-68324-628-2 (paperback)

Library of Congress Cataloging-in-Publication Data

Names: Ermine, Will, 1888-1979, author.
Title: Plundered range / Will Ermine.
Description: Center Point Large Print edition. | Thorndike, Maine :
    Center Point Large Print, 2017.
Identifiers: LCCN 2017045091| ISBN 9781683246244
    (hardcover : alk. paper) | ISBN 9781683246282 (pbk. : alk. paper)
Subjects: LCSH: Western stories. | Large type books.
Classification: LCC PS3507.R1745 P58 2017 2017 |
    DDC 813/.54—dc23
LC record available at https://lccn.loc.gov/2017045091

# Contents

# Plundered Range

# Chapter 1

## OUTLAW BLOOD

Race Cullyer studied the vicious gray horse in the corral with steady eyes, his lips compressed in a straight line.

The big stallion would not stand, whirling from one side to another with pounding hoofs; teeth bared in a wicked equine threat. He flung his blind-folded head with rage as the boys threw a busting-saddle on him and cinched it tight without ceremony. There appeared to be no fear in him; the trembling of his massive frame was that of savage readiness.

It was not a Diamond Bar horse. Race had never seen it before.

The buckaroos around the corral were watchful and expectant. The breaking of cow ponies was no new thing to them; yet one and all kept an eye on the proceedings as they murmured amongst themselves. They knew what was coming.

"You better pass up this hoss, Race," Spade McSween muttered warningly. "Fent Crocker's run in an outlaw on you. He done it apurpose. *He's* wise there's somethin' between you an' the boss's girl, an' he's out to git you. He's been foreman of the Diamond Bar so long he thinks he owns the place! Why play his game?"

Spade was Race Cullyer's partner, a grizzled, unlovely, club-footed puncher of forty.

Race shook his head. "I'm not playin' his game," he answered in a tone that precluded argument. "It's his mistake if he thinks so!" His glance slanted to the blunt, preoccupied foreman who stood across the corral.

"All right, Cullyer!" the latter called shortly. "Let's see if you c'n top off this big devil!"

The lean, hard wrangler entered the corral and strode through the dust toward the stallion, with set face and flapping bat-wing chaps. He looked neither to the right nor left, his whole mind fixed on the battle before him; yet he was conscious of old Luke Hamlin, the owner of the Diamond Bar, sitting with his daughter Fox on the top bar of the corral and watching interestedly.

With a minimum of waste motion, Race grasped the hackamore, inserted his foot in the stirrup, and rose to the saddle. The two men who held the horse's head sprang away as Race hit the leather. And none too soon. The maddened stallion stood rock-still for a realizing instant; then exploded into action.

The muscles in the powerful haunches bunched and snapped like steel springs. The big head swung around, eyes rolling redly, teeth snapping. Race slapped it down. The gray went into convulsions of bucking, sun-fishing, crow-hopping, and a dozen other dizzy, pitching tricks designed to snap the rider's back or dislodge him from his tenacious seat in the saddle.

Fent Crocker stood with feet wide-spread, an inscrutable look on his flinty face, watching the contest without emotion. Spade took time to shoot a glare of anger and contempt at him. Then the puncher's eyes were glued once more to the stallion.

The gray was fighting for domination with every ounce of his tremendous strength, and every throb of his wild heart. First the flaunting mane, and then the sweating, hard-muscled haunches, flashed in the sun as the stallion swapped ends in stiff-legged, spine-wrenching, head-snapping hops.

"Stay with 'im, cowboy!"

The buckaroos were yelling and waving their hats, hanging on to the corral bar; rooting for Race. Not one of them but would have hesitated to fork the horse, had they been in his shoes.

He hung on with clamped knees, his hat pulled down to his brows, his eyes mere slits in the clean-cut, determined face. He brought down the waving quirt with a slap, and his belligerent mount responded with a renewed and tireless violence.

Twice the stallion thudded to the ground and attempted to roll. Each time Race slipped nimbly off, rewarding the horse as he rose once more to the saddle with a discouraging rake of the spurs.

Fox Hamlin pounded the corral rail under her with clenched hands, stopping only when she realized what she was doing. She was small and vital, just past twenty; neat in the jacketed riding suit she wore. Her auburn hair escaped in curled tendrils from under the broad brim of her pearl gray Stetson. Her cheeks, above the firm, characteristic Hamlin chin, were flushed. Her blue eyes glowed with exultation in the combat she watched, and at the same time, with something very like indignation.

Race would not let the gray pause for an instant, raking him always to new frenzy. The stallion tried deliberately to kill him in any possible way. It was only the puncher's lightning quickness that prevented his being crushed against the logs of the corral.

When it began to dawn on the outlaw that he had met his master, he went berserk. Without warning he rose screaming on hind legs and sprang toward the corral fence as though he would crash through it. A gasp went up as the buckaroos saw that Fox Hamlin and old Luke were squarely in his path.

A look of horror dawned on Luke Hamlin's face. The cigar he had been chewing went flying. He was a big man, on the downhill side of sixty; but there was nothing slow in his movements as he went sidewise over the rail, scrambling to get out of the way. He yelled an unintelligible warning to Fox as he did so.

Race Cullyer saw the danger as quickly as anyone. He saw also that Fox had swung around, to leap backward off the fence—when the skirt of her riding jacket caught on a rough snag and held her fast. Frantically she fought to rip it loose, without result.

A roar went up from the watching buckaroos. Battling the enraged stallion, Race was tight-lipped. Every ounce of his strength was not enough to bring down the iron jaw of the gray, or alter its course. With clear intention, almost before he had had time to think, he took a desperate chance. Standing clear of the saddle, he threw his body to one side, yanking down on the hackamore in the hope that it would swerve the horse as he fell.

His last instant of clear sight took in a vision of Fox's white face, brave but hopeless. Then Race was falling. His back struck one of the corral poles a jarring blow. The outlaw reeled on its hind legs, pivoted slightly, and snapped the hackamore from Race's hands to pound away along the fence. Only by a miracle had its slashing hoofs missed the puncher's prone form.

The buckaroos went into action in an instant. Several of them cornered the stallion, while Spade leaped over and helped Race to his feet.

The latter was badly shaken up, but no bones were broken.

Luke Hamlin, angry and disheveled, was swearing at his foreman in round oaths as he stamped up and down outside the corral. Fox had succeeded in releasing herself, and was trying to quiet her father. Apparently she had sustained no great shock, although she was well aware of the peril she had escaped so narrowly.

"Dammit, Race—that's enough!" Spade protested disgustedly. "Now you *know* that hoss is an outlaw! Leave it go to hell!"

Shaking his head to clear it of the shock of his fall, Race was dogged. He looked up without answering as Fent Crocker came forward, with his employer's objurgations echoing behind him.

"Better lay off the gray, Cullyer," Crocker advised gruffly. "It's wilder'n I figured it. I don't want to break no necks here."

Eyeing him levelly, Race slowly shook his head. "I'm goin' to ride that stallion, Crocker!"

Fent stared at him, nonplussed. Then he shrugged. "Hop to it," he consented briefly. "It's your funeral!"

Spade McSween protested loudly, to no avail. Race walked to the stallion, which the buckaroos had roped, and flung himself into the saddle in a sharp, decisive manner.

"Let him go," he commanded grimly.

The fight that ensued was destined to make

history on the Nevada range. The stallion played every trick in the bag, but he had already lost out. Ten minutes later, Race signed for the gate to be thrown open. The stallion shot through it like an arrow, and in another minute was out of sight across the range.

Still angered by his experience, Luke Hamlin turned and stalked toward the Diamond Bar ranch house, blowing to himself. Fox hesitated until he disappeared around the bunkhouse, and then turned on Fent Crocker with flashing eyes.

"How does it happen that you're running outlaws in on the boys, these days, Mr. Crocker?" she asked flatly. "Is saddle stock so scarce that you can't find anything else?"

A frown crossed the foreman's broad forehead.

"Outlaw?" he grunted. "The gray's no outlaw. He's a leetle rough, maybe. The boys'll knock off the edges, an' he'll make a good cow pony." His tone, as always with her, was on the defensive.

"The boys?" she echoed bitingly. "Who except Race Cullyer could you have gotten to tackle the horse?"

Fent stared at her, stilled.

"I don't believe there's any doubt in your mind that the stallion is an outlaw!" the girl went on coldly. "What you can have against the boys that persuaded you to buy him, is beyond me!" Her eyes were dangerously bright.

Crocker stubbornly stuck to his stand. "A

15

man can make a mistake, once in a while," he contended bluntly.

"Then you didn't *know* the gray was an outlaw?" Fox persisted. "You didn't bring him here for a purpose?"

"No," was all Fent would answer. But the way in which she had put her question made his veins crawl with smouldering anger. What did she think he was up to, anyway? Hadn't he looked after the interests of the Diamond Bar for over fifteen years to the best of his, or anybody else's ability?

"So she thinks I'm pickin' on Race, eh?" he muttered to himself as she walked away. "I'll have to correct that impression, an' not lose no time about it!"

But he knew also that he must cover his own position. Disliking Cullyer for his stern conquest of the gray outlaw, he liked still less the effect of the affair on the Hamlins.

Crocker wasted no time in heated recriminations of Race, however. He knew he must speedily tear down the puncher's prestige; subtly but surely discredit the other by some ingenious means— make his judgment look particularly poor, if possible—at the same time that he appeared to entrust him with responsibility. Could he manage it? Fent spent an anxious hour in thought. Before he dismissed the subject, he felt he had devised just the set of circumstances he required.

He kept out of Race's way for the present, biding his time. It was Spade who met the puncher at the corrals on his return with the gray outlaw. The club-foot waited until Race had turned the weary stallion loose, and then accosted him soberly.

"Race, this is a dang muss we're into here," he began. "You can see Crocker's hand in what happened today! Why not ride away from here an' forget it?"

"Crocker don't worry me," Race replied flatly. He moved stiffly as they walked toward the bunkhouse.

"Well—he worries me!" Spade countered. "I'll tie into that hombre if he don't lay off . . . Race, why not chuck it? It's comin' on fall. We'll hit south for the winter again. What d'you say?"

Race was gazing absently in the direction of the ranch house, bowered in cottonwoods—a scene of rural magnificence, unusual in the cow country. Spade knew he was thinking about Fox Hamlin.

"I say no," he answered shortly. "I expect to see this thing through, Spade!" There was no harshness in his decision; only inflexible purpose. He had come to certain conclusions about Fent Crocker which demanded consideration.

Spade cursed in his throat and reluctantly gave over.

That evening Crocker approached Race in

the bunkhouse with an offhanded proposal that sounded like amends for the afternoon.

"I'm sendin' you up to the Reserve with some of the boys, to bring down the stock, Cullyer," he said. "Our permits're about run out. I don't want to overplay my hand up there. . . . You'll take half-a-dozen hands." He named those he wanted to go. "Start in the mornin', an' begin gatherin' the stuff. I'll see you up there 'bout day after tomorrow."

"Okay," Race answered, in his usual voice. Inwardly he was wondering if he had made a mistake about the foreman. Something warned him to remain on the alert, however.

Crocker talked a few minutes longer, in his disarming, absent manner, before he left the bunkhouse.

He was careful, later, to inform old Luke of what he had done, in the presence of Fox. Hamlin nodded abstractedly, chewing his cigar. His daughter gazed at the foreman without an expression on her face. Turning away, Fent prided himself that he had not only allayed the girl's suspicions, but had so arranged matters that she and Race Cullyer would be far apart as well.

"We'll jest see how much of a hero he is when he gets back!" he told himself, nodding his head firmly.

# Chapter II

## TROUBLE AT SQUAW FLAT

With the exception of the lofty Calico Mountains, edging the Idaho line across the north, the Santa Rosa Forest Reserve dominates in height the surrounding country. Watered by the feeders of the North Fork of the Little Humboldt, and by those of Martin's Creek; hemmed in on the east by the Owyhee Desert, and on the west by the Black Rock; unencumbered by heavy forest growth, the Reserve offers an ideal grazing range.

Every summer it supports thousands of cattle and sheep, for between the hillside tangles of mahogany bush and patches of aspen, and the stands of dwarf pine on the heights, the forage is excellent.

Race Cullyer and the six cowboys arrived on the Reserve, and the work of gathering the Diamond Bar steers went forward without hitch, although it was not easy. The cattle had ranged on the high hills long enough to feel at home. They had no intention of being moved if they could help it. Nevertheless they were hazed out of the hollows and brush patches with scant ceremony.

Fent Crocker put in an appearance on the

morning of the second day, and looked over the growing herd.

"You ought to have 'em rounded up by sometime tomorrow," he told Race crisply. "I'll be back later today, an' tell you when to start 'em down the trail."

Race nodded. Though it had not been said, he understood that Crocker meant to make sure when the summit trail to the lower range would be open. It would necessitate visiting several of the distant sheep camps, but apparently the foreman chose to make that a part of his work.

Fent had no more to say, sending his pony away at a trot. Race watched him ride out of sight over a swell, and then turned back to his work.

Crocker did not show up again until late afternoon. Riding around the herd with Race, he estimated the number of steers yet to be gathered.

"You've got all but a hundred or so," he commented. "Ought to be done tomorrow, an' that'll be just right. Cullyer, I want you to start 'em for home by evening. That'll get you down to the Diamond Bar late the next day." He gave a few more terse directions, to which Race listened in silence, and then nodded.

"Don't hold over to mornin', now," Crocker repeated as he made ready to leave.

"All right, Crocker," Race agreed, although he knew it meant a hard night's work for them all, on top of a strenuous day.

The buckaroos were less amiable in their acceptance of the foreman's orders. They listened incredulously, around the fire that evening, while Race told them what must be done. Then they exploded into disgusted protest. Spade McSween was loudest of all.

"Where does Crocker get off with that stuff?" he demanded angrily. "He knows it don't have to be done that way!"

He twitched his clubbed foot irritably, turning away. That leg was slightly shorter than the other, so that he walked with a slightly rolling gait as he went to procure his tobacco from a saddle pocket.

"Wal, all I got to say is, Crocker does about as he damn well pleases!" Baldy Crebo snorted.

"He must be fixin' it so's we won't meet up with no sheep down on the Squaw Flat crossin'," Stub Varian volunteered. "Maybe Crocker *don't* give a damn about us; but he pays attention to his business."

"That's what comes of lettin' sheep into a country at all," Win Flood put in sourly. "Wouldn't be none here if *I* had anythin' to say. Paradise Valley's half-full of broncho grass already!" Win was notably bitter in his resentment against sheep and all they connoted.

"Well, we've got our orders and we'll carry them out," Race cut short their bickering.

They subsided, grumbling. Saddle-worn and

21

irritable, they were soon in their blankets, and were abroad early the following morning.

The last of the Diamond Bar steers were rounded up by mid-afternoon. After a hasty meal—the last they would get for some time— the buckaroos started the herd down the long trail.

It was the most difficult task they had yet attempted. The wild steers broke back repeatedly. Only by dint of strenuous riding did the men manage at length to get them moving.

"We'll push them well along while it's light," Race told Spade, riding near at hand. "If we tire 'em a little now, it will simplify matters after dark."

Spade nodded agreement. For more than three years now he had followed the younger man with unwavering fidelity. He had come to the Diamond Bar with Race, and meant to leave with him. In the meantime he was a tireless companion in fun or trouble.

If this attitude irked Race at times, he gave no sign of it. He presented always to the homely puncher, in whose devotion there was nothing of the dog-like, an aspect of uncritical amity tempered with understanding.

The westering sun cast long shadows across the slopes and made gigantic caricature of men and beasts. Busy as he was, Race found time to savor the spirit of the hour. The blazing yellow patches of aspen on the canyon slopes, in their autumnal dress; the intense indigo of the sky above the Calico peaks to the north, and the thin, keen atmosphere, touched with renewed vigor a chord in him that awaited just these signals. He snapped into the work of pushing the drive along with an energy which exceeded that of any other man in the outfit.

Evening came and passed, and the cattle moved on into the darkness. The grassy swells were left behind. Rocks grated under the hoofs of the steers.

From the higher levels, the Forest Reserve drops down until its southern portion is no more than an inhospitable desert, flinty, grassless, and littered with dwarf sage. Through this vast expanse the cattle followed the trails past the rocky, waterless gorges.

The heat of the boiling sun lingered in the rocks. Long after midnight, Race felt the warm breath on his face. The steers kicked up clouds of dust on which the rising moon glinted weirdly.

The buckaroos were fagged by the time the herd reached the entrance to the rocky defile of Indian Creek. It was the only passage through to the summit of the Cottonwood Range, below which lay the Diamond Bar. The worse of the parched and dusty desert trek had been traversed. The first light of dawn streaked the eastern sky.

"Wal, this begins to look like home," Baldy

Crebo commented to Race, wiping the grime from his weathered face. "We'll soon be waterin' at the flat."

Race made no direct rejoinder to this.

"Baldy—you, Win Flood, and Spade come on with me," he directed briefly. "We'll go on up to the point and stay there. No need of flankin' the steers in the canyon."

They pushed ahead, glad to be out of the heat and dust of the herd after the long night hours.

The Indian Creek trail was a wide ledge along the side of the canyon, dry at this point. The morning light had strengthened so that they could see fairly well, and Race gazed ahead for his first glimpse of Squaw Flat. The canyon wound too sharply to afford lengthy vision.

"Man, this is what I call *easy!*" Spade remarked. "I've heard of makin' a bed out of a saddle, but there was times last night when I thought mine was a—" He paused, glancing sharply at Race. "What's the matter, Race?" he broke off.

The latter was examining marks in the dust.

"Sheep," he grunted shortly. He stepped out of the saddle for a closer look. When he rose, there was a hard glint in his eyes. "Fresh, too!" he added, grimly.

Win Flood swore angrily at the suggestion. "Damned if I don't see them things in my sleep!" he jerked out.

"You'll see them wide awake, if I'm not

24

mistaken!" Race came back at him. "We're within half-a-mile of Squaw Flat. They're likely there now!"

They began to ride forward at a mended pace. Behind them, the steers, catching the scent of water, pressed ahead more rapidly.

When Race got a clear view of Squaw Flat at last, he saw that which made him curse heartily. Below the canyon trail, the irregular, grassy flat was massed with sheep. Several herders were in sight, Basques by the look of them, staring up the trail and calling excitedly to one another.

"Dammit all—look at that!" Baldy Crebo burst out. "Race, what're we goin' to do now?"

"Block the herd!" Race directed swiftly, wheeling in his saddle. "We've got to hold it till the sheep are out of the way! Don't lose no time about it!"

Already the foremost steers were in sight, massed and thirst-maddened, rushing forward blindly.

"You can't stop them!" Win Flood bawled.

"Do as I say!" Race thundered.

The punchers turned to face the cattle, rowelling their ponies back and forth, and waving ropes while they shouted at the top of their voices. Race jerked his six-gun out and fired into the dust. In a moment the others were imitating him.

The lead steers broke, faltering. They were not ready to give up, however; seeking a way through, tossing their horns and bellowing in frenzy. Behind them, the onrushing herd piled up in a resistless tide. As they massed, milling, they were crowded to the lip of the trail.

"Hell's hinges!" Spade exploded. "There goes a steer clean over the edge, Race! Half the stock'll be dead on the rocks if we try to hold 'em!"

"We've *got* to hold them!" Race snapped fiercely.

Despite their best efforts, a bull broke past and raced toward the creek bellowing. It ploughed into the sheep, tossing the smaller animals to right and left, crippling several. Behind it, two dead ewes lay with broken necks. The terrified bleats of the others mingled with the continuous uproar of the cattle.

The cries of the Basques rose in a frenzy of hatred and vengeance. One of them had a rifle. He began to pump slugs at the bull, and at the second vicious crack, his victim leaped forward with a scream, to fall prostrate, kicking.

The punchers whirled to face the flat. Win Flood's face was a picture of knotted rage.

"Damn you, take that, bosco!" he howled, and snapped a shot from his .45 at the herder with the rifle.

"Lay off!" Race blazed at him, reaching out to grasp his arm, and almost dragging him out of the saddle. "What do you think you're doin', Flood?"

Win stared at him in sudden heat. "Doin'!" he echoed. "I'm tryin' to ventilate them blasted—!"

"You're not doin' anything of the sort!" Race cut him off sharply. "Suppose you let me handle this!"

Win cursed in his exasperation. "What's the matter with you, Race? The damn skunks're shootin' our bulls! Here—look at this, if you don't think it's serious!" He pawed excitedly at his clothing. Race saw where a slug had torn through shirt and vest narrowly missing the buckaroo's vitals.

"Never mind!" he retorted. "We're not going to have a shoot-out over it, an' that goes!"

Flood turned away muttering.

The sheep had been effectually stampeded. Already two-thirds of the flock had raced up the far trail, or the rocky slopes beyond the flat. Many of them had fallen from the trail ledge as the steers had done, and lay in a broken, bleeding mass at the bottom of the gorge.

Race estimated that there were half-a-dozen herders, although he could not be sure. Several of them had rushed after the sheep, trying to head them off; and only two remained in the flat.

Kneeing his pony forward, Race rode to meet the middle-aged Basque with the rifle.

"What are you doin' here?" he demanded, his eyes flashing.

The dark-visaged man watched him narrowly, his small eyes gleaming under the shapeless hat-brim. He fingered his rifle restlessly.

"*Madre de Dios*, you ask that!" he ejaculated harshly. "What about you, señor? You know *we* are here!"

Race watched him closely.

"What makes you think I knew?" he snapped.

The other gesticulated violently. "Don't we tell Señor Crocker? *He* know we are here!"

Race began to see the light. It did not improve his temper. "Who are you?" he asked, his face hard.

The Basque hesitated. "Mateo Madriaga," he muttered. And when Race jerked his head toward the young Basque near by: "Ramon—my son."

"And the sheep?"

"Fontana's."

Race nodded, thinking swiftly. "When you tell Fontana what happened here, don't forget to tell him you shot one of our bulls—and that we lost as much as you did, and likely more. Get that?" There was a lash of warning in his tone.

Madriaga's answer was only a suspicious nod.

"All right! Now get the hell out of here pronto!" Race went on sharply.

The inscrutable eyes met his momentarily, and drifted back to Win Flood. Then the Basques turned sullenly away.

The buckaroos had allowed the steers to come forward to the waters of Chief Creek, which here entered the Indian Creek gorge. In five minutes Squaw Flat was jammed with Diamond Bar cattle.

# Chapter III

## CROCKER MARKS TIME

"Damn it all, Race—Crocker knowed this was goin' to happen here!" Spade McSween exclaimed angrily, riding forward to join the other while the cattle were slaking their thirst. "You can't tell me any different! . . . You heard what that bosco claimed. Nine times out of ten, I wouldn't believe a word one of them coyotes said—but this time I'm willin' to stake plenty that Crocker is playin' you dirt."

Race nodded, his face unrelenting.

"Crocker knew, all right!" he agreed dryly. "I know too. I'm goin' to tell him all about it! . . . I've got him figured pretty well by this time," he went on after a moment. "I wasn't sure before, but things are droppin' into place too regular to be accidental!"

"Shore!" Spade rejoined strongly. "You see what I see. Would he have it in for you, if it didn't mean somethin' to him to get you out of the way? . . . He wants to get rid of you, Race; or anybody else that might be a real help to Miss Fox between now an' the time old Luke cashes his chips—an' maybe afterward too. I seen that long ago."

Race had seen it too, but he hesitated in his

decision, for it was a serious charge to make against any man. Yet the longer he studied it, the more certain he became, that Fent Crocker had designs on the Diamond Bar ranch.

Time was when it had been a prosperous ranch; but that was before Luke Hamlin's love of his daughter Fox had led him to extremes. It was on her account that, during her last year at Mills College, Luke had foresworn living in the uncared-for and unprepossessing old Diamond Bar ranch house, which most nearly suited his tastes, and had at no little expense to himself converted the place into the scene of opulence it now was.

Crocker had protested, to no avail. He had watched the stock on the ranch dwindle until it was no longer a financial success.

Luke Hamlin was failing of late years. The time when he would have seen to it that this condition was changed, had gone. He hung on, trying almost childishly to please his daughter, and left the management of the brand virtually to the foreman. It would have taken a stronger character than Crocker's to ignore the temptation. He meant in time to own the ranch on which he had worked so long.

Race Cullyer saw it all clearly.

"Wait till we get back to the ranch," he decided. "I'll speak my little piece, make no mistake about it!"

The other buckaroos were gathered a little apart, arguing. Win Flood could be heard declaring what he was going to do to the next Basque who crossed his trail. All of them realized the significance of the encounter with the sheepherders. They watched Race as though asking themselves what he intended to do next.

The Diamond Bar herd was driven on its way as soon as the steers had satisfied their thirst. Arriving at the Cottonwood summit just as the sun flashed out of the east, Race beheld the broad sweep of Paradise Valley, swathed in purple veils and barred with the shadows of the Santa Rosa heights. Down there, the ranches dotted the land in miniature. Far to the south, Winnemucca Peak caught the light. Elsewhere, the plains stretched away to vague, illimitable horizons. It was a dreamy, peaceful scene, but it held also a promise of strife, and the sure stress of problems to be met. Race's face was lean and hard as he started down the trail behind the cattle.

The Diamond Bar range was reached shortly after midday. Race headed at once for the ranch.

He found Fent Crocker at his own cottage. The foreman paused in the door upon hearing the rapid pound of hoofs, and turned an inscrutable face as Race drew up and slid out of the saddle.

"Crocker, I want to talk to you!"

Fent said nothing, his glance sharpening.

"We ran into sheep this mornin' at Squaw

Flat," Race went on in swift, level tones, "after you made so sure we'd get there on time! A few sheep were killed—and we lost three steers over the edge of the canyon, and a bull shot by the Basques! . . . Damn you, Crocker, you planted that on me!"

The foreman controlled himself admirably, though his face darkened.

"Watch your tongue, Cullyer!" he snapped.

"*You* watch it—and the rest of me, while you're about it!" Race challenged. "Damn you, you're a rotten skunk, and I want you to know I know it!"

A flush of rage showed under Crocker's saddle-colored visage.

"Why don't you quit, then, if you don't like the way I run things around here?" he flung back.

The smile that twisted Race's lips had no humor in it. "No," he answered flatly. "Crocker, if I go off the Diamond Bar, it'll be because I'm fired off!"

Fent appeared about to retort, but he thought better of it. "Then see you keep a civil word for me, Cullyer, before I take it out of your hide!" he warned, his stare unwavering.

It was the crudest kind of a goad. Race chose to ignore it, grasping the foreman's shoulder and pulling him forward.

"Go ahead and fire me!" he defied instantly. "You don't dare, Crocker!—though it's plain enough you'd like to be rid of me! I seem to be standing in your way, for some reason! What's the idea?"

Fent jerked himself free, his dark eyes blazing with wrath. "You flatter yourself aplenty, mister!" he said dangerously. "If you crave to keep your job, close that trap of yours tight! And don't run away with the idea that I *won't* fire you!"

He stared vindictively for another moment, and then swung away. Race halted him.

"Hold on, Crocker! I'm not done with you!" he bit out. "I tell you, I've got the deadwood on you now! I'll land on you like a ton of rock if you don't walk a chalk line from here on out!"

He matched stares with the enraged foreman for a bare instant, before he gave the other a thrust that sent him lurching. Fent recovered, glared his wordless hatred, and stalked away.

"Yes, he'd fire me in a second, if he thought it wouldn't mean anything to anyone but himself and me," Race mused, as he watched the other's departure. He knew he had penetrated the weak point in Crocker's armor. The more ugly Fent had got, the less prepared he was to fight. Perhaps nothing Race could do would have made the foreman strike back. He had had the man against a wall, and he had driven the fact home so that he hoped it would stick. On the other hand, nothing could have been more certain proof of Crocker's guilt. He had been determined not to let Race force his hand. It marked him for a dangerous enemy.

Race saddled up a fresh pony, and rode away to his work. It was a surprise to him to run across Fox Hamlin on Spider Creek, although he had been thinking about her.

"Hello," she greeted him. "I see you've got down from the Reserve with the stock."

He assented, watching the lights play in her unruly hair.

She asked about the condition of the cattle. He answered her without making any mention of what had occurred at Squaw Flat.

Fox turned her pony in beside his without comment, and they rode on. Race gave himself over to the enjoyment of her companionship.

Meanwhile, Spade McSween rode in from the herd at his own gait. He arrived at the ranch house just after Race had left.

Spade was alive to what was in the air, but he had no idea what had taken place. Caring for his horse at the corrals, he watched the bunkhouse and the foreman's cottage with covert care. He saw nothing of Crocker then; and the longer he was kept in doubt, the more angry he became.

It was five minutes later, as he came around the corner of the saddle-shed with his rolling walk, that he almost bumped into the foreman. Fent's face was somber, his manner abrupt.

"So you're still alive, Crocker!" Spade met him contemptuously.

Fent halted, staring. "Damn you, McSween—!"

Spade's face went cold and deadly. "Crocker, yo're the rottenest hunk of humanity there is! The skunk's trick you put onto Race is mighty plain! Why he didn't kill you is beyond me—but I've a mind to!"

Crocker blew up. "You can't get away with that talk to me! Get off of this ranch, McSween!" His voice rose, hoarse and uncontrollable.

Spade crouched, hatred in every line of his body.

"I've got a license that says I'll stay on this ranch!" he bit out. He slapped his six-gun significantly. "If you think you can top it—show yore guts!"

Fent's broad, blunt face went white. "So you're a gunman, eh?" he snarled.

Spade took a long step forward and stared into the other's hard eyes.

"I'm a man!" he contradicted sarcastically. "It's plain there ain't no part of one about you!" With slow, deliberate words he set about blasting Crocker's soul, flaying him with searing invective.

"By God, I won't listen to you!" Fent burst out furiously, his voice trembling. "Get off the Diamond Bar, you hound!" he reiterated with a show of suppressed violence. "I'll give you till mornin'!" Swinging on his heel, he started off.

Spade grasped his shoulder and spun him around. "We're doin' business here an' now!" he grated. So that there could be no misunderstanding his meaning, he laid his work-hardened fingers alongside Crocker's jaw in a stinging slap. "Won't nothin' make you fight, you coyote?"

Crocker blanched, quivering. "Don't you drive me too far, McSween!" he raged. "I don't want no part of your game, but I'll see you off this ranch if it's the last thing I do!"

Spade sneered scathingly. "No damn wonder Race didn't finish you!" he rasped. "He couldn't shoot any man like the rat you are! But I ain't got his scruples, Crocker! . . . Go tell the boss! Tell her I threatened you! Tell the sheriff the same! It'll be the quickest ticket to hell you ever bought!"

Crocker was so beside himself that his voice was unrecognizable. "Take off that gun!" he croaked. "By God, I'll break you!" The veins in his forehead were taut to bursting.

Spade laughed at him, a wolf's laugh. Crocker abruptly whirled and burst from the place almost running. Spade let him go, his eyes slitted, his lips curled.

Far on the range, Race knew nothing of this. Half-an-hour later, having met Fox, he had forgot even his own ire against the foreman for the time being.

That evening, however, he was recalled to himself abruptly when Crocker came to him where he unsaddled the ponies at the corral, and said shortly:

"The old man wants you, up to the house."

"All right," Race responded unemotionally.

Fent's glance slid over his features calculatingly, and then withdrew. If he had expected Race to show irritation at the summons, he was disappointed.

Race found his employer in the patio of the ranch house. He was alone.

"Cullyer, what in hell're you up to, anyway?" he demanded testily. "Crocker tells me you lost three steers an' a bull comin' down from the Reserve! Dammit man, I—"

"Did he tell you the rest of it?" Race interposed coolly.

Hamlin paused to stare at him. "Rest of what?" he barked.

Race told him in terse phrases what had occurred. He did not neglect to add the fact that Crocker had been on the Reserve himself, and had given exact directions as to the time of the drive.

"That's no answer!" old Luke blustered, when he had finished. "Crocker told *me* he went to the sheepmen! He claims they changed their minds to suit themselves! . . . What've you got to say for *yore* end of this fool play?"

Race held himself in with an effort.

"Nothing," he countered, "except that it could have been plenty worse, Hamlin, if I hadn't given a damn! . . . I tried my best to steer around a run-in with the sheep. I don't know whether I succeeded or not. What would you have done?" This firm tone surprised old Luke. He chewed his cigar nervously, turning it in his lips.

"Wal, I *think* I'd have brought that herd down without losin' a head, if I'd had to kill every sheep in Humboldt County!" he got out finally, with heavy sarcasm. "I'm some dubious about you," he went on more strongly. "After the play you made last week, I had you marked down for more sense!" He rambled on angrily, venting his exasperation. Race listened with what patience he could muster.

Suddenly old Luke stopped, staring at him piercingly from under heavy lids. "Why don't you say somethin'?" he shot out.

"I've said it," Race answered shortly.

"Wal, git on out of here, then!" Hamlin exploded, throwing his cigar down. "And Cullyer—" he added, before the other turned away; "hereafter, a little more ridin' an' a little less lady-killin' will suit me fine!"

He had saved this shot until the last; and walking back to the bunkhouse with set jaws, Race knew that it had been as much Crocker's doing as anything.

"He's got plenty to answer for," he told himself grimly. "And if he don't bring it to me, I'll take it to him!"

But as he rolled in his bunk that night, too wearied to sleep, he wondered from what direction the foreman's subtle attack would come next. There was little doubt that it would come; none whatever that Race would grasp the opportunity it afforded with firm grip.

It was difficult to read enmity into the foreman's next move at first glance. Two days later he stopped Race in the ranch yard and said gruffly:

"Cullyer, throw what you want in your war-bag tonight. I'm sendin' you, McSween, Stub Varian, an' Crebo out to the Dutch John Creek line camp in the mornin'. You'll be straw-boss."

"Okay," Race answered briefly. Inwardly, however, his thoughts were in a whirl. "Four men!" he exclaimed to himself as Fent walked away. "What can he want with so many out there? Two would be too many!"

It was just possible that Crocker had received some sign that led him to expect hostilities as a repercussion of the affair with the sheepmen at Squaw Flat. Race thought he saw light in another direction, however, when he told Fox Hamlin of his instructions, and watched her face fall.

"How long will you be out there?" she asked.

"I don't know."

"Well, but that's—" She paused. "Maybe we could—meet somewhere?" she went on, watching him.

"We've done it before," he smiled. "But Fox, your father has told me he'd just as soon I stayed away from you."

"Do you want to?" she countered evenly.

"Why, no!" he answered quickly. "I was thinking of you. You know how I feel about that."

Fox relented. "Shall we say at the Pinnacles, on Saturdays—?"

"—At sunset," he rejoined.

"But then the Pinnacles are off our range, aren't they? That is better for me, but what if anything were to happen while you are away?"

"I'll risk it," he said shortly. "If Fontana's herders get over the line, I'll know it soon enough!"

The line camp at Dutch John Creek was a tumbledown cabin ten miles or more away from the home ranch. The range line, following the Creek, was here broken and irregular. The four buckaroos kept a strict watch, and nothing happened. It was a welcome change for Race to slip away on Saturday and meet Fox at the lofty, lonely granite Pinnacles.

It puzzled him to learn that nothing out of the ordinary had occurred at the ranch. He had been waiting to learn the latest developments in the vicinity of Fent Crocker.

41

When a second weekend arrived, and Fox had nothing of importance to tell him, Race confessed himself stumped. He divined with grudging admiration the depth of the foreman's patience, and settled down to a process of waiting the other out.

It was no easy task. When Saturday drew near once more, he found himself tensed for the news he more than half expected. Immediately the day had dawned, he was impatient for the evening.

Events forestalled him from an unexpected quarter. It was not yet mid-morning, and Race, Spade McSween and Baldy Crebo were smoking while they hung out the blankets to air, when a thunder of wildly driven hoofs drew them to a corner of the cabin. Stub Varian had returned, hours ahead of his time.

"What is it?" Race demanded, pushing forward.

"We're in for it!" Stub exclaimed breathlessly, sliding out of the saddle. "I was crossin' the creek, five miles down, when I heard a shot, across in the breaks. I rode over—saw a puncher a-foggin'. It was Win Flood! I went on—found scattered sheep—then a dead bosco. Shot plumb center! Boys, Flood has went an' perforated Mateo Madriaga, as he threatened! Now there'll be hell to pay!"

# Chapter IV

## AT THE PINNACLES

For a moment, the silence of surprise held the three buckaroos. Baldy Crebo broke it.

"Win Flood!" he ejaculated. "He *swore* he'd knock off a bosco! Now he's done it! By God, we'll hear plenty from this!"

He left the group with an intent manner. A moment later, he came out of the cabin working the lever of a rifle.

"Wal, where do we commence, Race?" he demanded.

"Hold on, now! We've got to figure this out!" Race swung back to Stub. He questioned the puncher tersely:

"Varian, did you see any other herders over there?"

Stub hadn't. "But they'll be over the line quick enough!" he supplemented grimly.

Race went on keenly, fixing the facts in his mind. While he was putting his queries, Baldy Crebo and Spade were hustling up their ponies. Spade threw a saddle on Race's mount.

"Not much to go on," the straw-boss commented briefly, when Stub had told all he knew. "We won't waste any time wonderin'!" He swung

43

up on the pony which the club-footed puncher led forward. "Baldy, you and Stub take the north line! Spade and I'll follow the creek down! . . . Let's ride!"

They rode away from the line camp in a whirl of dust. In a moment all four punchers were watching the range boundary.

The sheep range of Fontana, the Basque, paralleled the Diamond Bar for a number of miles along Dutch John Creek. Race and Spade scanned the broken land across the creek for the first signs of activity. The former had no doubt there would be stern reprisals for Win Flood's violent act.

No one was to be seen. Fontana's range lay empty and noncommittal. The sun reached its meridian and began to descend. Still Dutch John Creek remained silent, ominously peaceful under the watchful scrutiny of the Diamond Bar men.

Race had said almost nothing for hours, although Spade tried to get him to talk. He was thinking about his tryst with Fox Hamlin for that night.

Spade knew what was worrying him. "Don't look like the boscos'll git goin' before night," he ventured off-handedly. "They'll be out then—an' we'll be on the hop!"

Race grunted. "Somethin' *would* have to come up just at this time!" he muttered, his face bleak.

Spade stole a glance at his face. "Hell's goin'

to pop around here, pronto!" he went on. "Thing fer us to do is stick to our business, an' not fool around with—other things." He was gazing away as he spoke, and his voice was gruff. The significance of his words was far from casual.

It fell in so accurately with Race's own reflections that he swung on his companion, arrested. "What do you mean by that?" he demanded roughly.

Spade squirmed around in his saddle. "Don't go jumpin' onto me that-a-way! I knowed a man once that just wouldn't stick to his own. . . . Why, take Win Flood!" he broke off evasively. "There's a swell example!"

"Speak what's on your mind!" Race cut him short, pinning him with a keen stare.

"Now—Race, I know where it is you go off to, Saturday nights," Spade broke out frankly. "An' if I'm able to find out, somebody else may know! . . . I don't want you to go tonight!"

Race's temper did not improve under this appeal. "Have you been following me?" he snapped.

"No!" McSween denied flatly.

Race subsided into angry silence, and it was several minutes before he glanced up again.

"I've got to go!" he relented finally, his brows knit. "If it was just myself, I'd pass it up—but Spade, there's somebody else in danger. I *can't* stay away tonight!"

45

"We-ll," McSween hung on, "why not let me foller this time? Just to cover you."

"No," Race demurred, shaking his head, "I'll ride alone, and fast!"

They did not refer to the subject again, but the straw-boss could not get it out of his mind. Nor did his apprehensions grow less as the afternoon waned and no hostile men put in an appearance across Dutch John Creek.

Back at the camp, Crebo and Stub Varian met them with questioning eyes. Race shook his head negatively as he and McSween drew up and dismounted.

Crebo and Varian rode away shortly afterwards, and Race was free to start for the Pinnacles. Anxiety in his eyes, Spade watched him ride away through the changing glow of the evening hour.

Race set his pony to a steady, unhurried gait. Although he had nearly a dozen miles to cover, he guessed that Fox might be later tonight than usual. She must know that there was no telling who might be abroad on the range. Dangerous as their rendezvous was, there would be some safety in the cover of the desert night.

The Pinnacles were not upon land claimed by anyone, for around them the soil was barren and worthless. The spot was not far removed from Fontana's northern boundary, however. Fox would have to ride across several miles of the outermost fringe of the sheep range to reach it.

Night had fallen when Race reached the trysting-place. Fox was not there. As time passed and she did not come, his fears began to mount. Had she been unable to get away this time? Had she come at the usual hour, waited, and then returned to the Diamond Bar? Or had she been stopped on the range by some revengeful minion of Fontana?

He stirred restlessly while these questions tortured him. He did not know whether to wait longer or not. Ten o'clock came, and eleven, and Fox did not arrive. The moon rose, casting a pale illumination. He was girding himself to follow her trail across the sheep range, no matter what the cost, when a rapid patter of hoofs drew his attention. He halooed lowly, and listened with bated breath.

"Here," Fox's voice came to him through the luminous darkness. "Race, is that you?"

They were together in a moment.

"You shouldn't have come!" he breathed his relief. "I began to wonder what had happened to you! Did you have trouble?"

"Such a time as I had, getting away!" she exclaimed. "It seems as though everyone were out on the range tonight. Dad didn't want me to leave the house. I only managed to slip out late on the pretext of visiting Sarah Finch for an hour!"

"What is going on?" he demanded, grasping her bridle chain. "Do Crocker and your father know about Madriaga's death? What will they do?"

Fox appeared agitated. "So that was the poor fellow's name? . . . No one seemed to know. Win Flood came in at noon with a story of unwarranted attack upon him; he said he had to shoot a man in getting away, but didn't think he was dead. Later Flood, Mr. Crocker and father had a conference. I don't know what was decided. I think father was for discharging Flood, but Mr. Crocker said we would have need of all the men we could get. He is riding around at top speed. He left the ranch shortly before myself tonight. I was mortally afraid we would meet! But I saw nothing of him."

"Has any word been sent to Fontana?" Race persisted seriously.

"I don't know." Fox shook her head, her eyes wide. "Race, what *can* come of it, if the attack on Flood was unprovoked?"

"The chances are, it wasn't," he answered soberly. He told her of Win Flood's part in the affair at Squaw Flat, and recalled the threats he had made later. "It looks as though Win had gone out of his way to make that good," he ended.

"But—that's criminal, inexcusable!" she exclaimed. "Is there a chance it will be considered purely a matter between the two men?"

"No, it will assume bigger proportions than that. Men will see in it another flare-up of the sheep and cattle feud. You know what that will mean."

"Then we are in danger right now!" she caught him up, her face white in the thin glow of the young moon.

He assented reluctantly. "We'll have to give up our meetings for the present. No sheepman would hesitate to fire on us. I don't believe we run any risk at this particular spot, but—"

His words were cut off by the startling crack of a rifle. Simultaneous with the echo of the shot on the rugged flank of the Pinnacles, a slug struck his saddle-horn a blow that staggered the pony, and ricocheted toward Fox with a scream. The girl gave an inarticulate cry and swayed backward.

Race was out of his saddle in a flash. He caught Fox's slumping form before she struck the ground, and released her heel from the stirrup. Blood ran down the side of her face in a glistening stream. Race laid her on her back at a level spot; and only then did he glance up in the direction from which the shot had come. His jaws were corded with wrath.

"Shot down without a chance!" he raged, gripping his six-gun. "That slug was meant for me; and now look what I've got her into! They've killed her!"

# Chapter V

## SPLIT TRAILS

After the spiteful crack of the one disastrous rifle shot, and Race Cullyer's low, despairing cry as he crouched over the still form of Fox Hamlin, silence enfolded the Pinnacles. A minute passed, and became five, and there was no renewal of the attack.

Race had no thought of leaving the girl's side, fierce as his desire was to hunt down the cowardly assassin and wipe him out. Evidently the other had been alone, a herder who had skulked away through the enigmatic night. The sickle moon, the weakness of whose light alone had saved Race's own life, would lend no practical aid in a pursuit. Precious time would be lost, that he could not spare.

For Race knew now, from a hasty examination, that Fox was not dead. If she could be gotten to a doctor at once she might live. The slug had struck the side of her head, inflicting a nasty scalp wound. The crude bandage, fashioned from her own clothing, with which Race swathed her head only partially staunched the flow of blood. But she was still breathing, slowly, heavily, as one does who is fighting for life.

There was only one thing for him to do, and that was to get her back to the Diamond Bar by the shortest possible route, regardless of peril to himself. He knew to the last jot the danger of an ambush or a running fight in crossing Fontana's domain. That would be bad enough. But when he thought of the look on Luke Hamlin's face when he heard the news— Sharply Race straightened as a further thought struck him.

"I've got to take her home and explain where she was, and *why!*" Swiftly the realization of his position thudded home. "I've got to explain to old Luke what I was doing a dozen miles off my own range, at a time like this!" he muttered dazedly. "That'll be bad!"

The fact that he had got Fox into this situation while paying secret court to her, did not escape him. He knew without taking thought what Luke Hamlin's reaction would be. It would mean an explosion—scathing criticism—discharge. Exactly what Fent Crocker wanted to happen to him!

Then hesitation left him. "It only means my job, my good name here—against Fox's life!" There could be no further question of the choice.

Swiftly he made ready for the start for the Diamond Bar, seeing to his guns, and leading his pony, the heaviest of the two, close to where Fox lay. "Her horse will have to find its own way home," he muttered, slapping the animal on its haunch. The mare snorted and kicked up her heels, the gravel clattering as she disappeared into the darkness.

Race gathered Fox's limp form in his arms and straightened up. Her smallness and lightness struck him poignantly. Nevertheless it was no easy undertaking to mount his pony with her without wrench or jolt. He finally accomplished it.

"Now," he told the roan, touching it with his knees. The pony started away at a fast walk. Race held the girl easily, gazing down at her still, white cheeks, on which her lashes lay like those of a child. A riot of emotions stormed in his breast. It was for her that he worried as he scanned the spacious emptiness about him, and forced the pony to greater speed. The roan broke into a choppy trot, and Race cursed in his throat as he pressed it on still faster to an even, gliding pace.

The trail left the open desert and wound through sage, over which the moon cast a ghostly effulgence that was more hindrance than help. Time and again he found himself narrowly watching some distant clump having the aspect of motionless horsemen. He was on Fontana's range by this time, and anything might happen. He pictured to himself how he would hold Fox with one arm, at need, leaving his other hand free for his six-gun.

It seemed that the roan pony's hoofs made twice the clatter they would have made in daylight. He was on edge before he had gone five miles. Though the night was cool, perspiration beaded his forehead.

It was close upon midnight when he entered the sheep range; one o'clock by the time he won across its fringe. He was just beginning to congratulate himself on the successful completion of a bold feat, when the night breeze wafted to him a sound that froze the blood in his veins and made him jerk the roan to a stand.

Taut with apprehension, he strove to pierce the night, without result. The thin moon had sunk until its pale light threw long, baffling shadows across the sage. There came to him again, however, that sound which he had first heard. He was able to distinguish the distant passage of several riders. Had they heard the echoing hoof-beats of the roan?

Five minutes ahead of Race, and pushing his pony hard, Fent Crocker heard those hoof-pounds also, but he did not stop. Changing his direction slightly, he drummed on toward his own range. His boldness stood him in good stead, for he was not followed.

Half-an-hour later the foreman circled the Diamond Bar and approached from the north. After caring hurriedly for his mount, he went down the path to the house. He had seen the light in the patio, where Luke Hamlin, knowing Fox was not in yet, waited restlessly.

"Where you been?" the rancher demanded sharply, as the two men met. "Seen anything of Fox?"

Crocker's quick glance of concern was almost genuine. "Isn't she home? I thought—" Then at old Luke's grunt, he quickly shunted away from the possibility of a slip: "I been over on the South Fork." After a moment's silence, he reverted: "Where'd she go? Anything I c'n do?"

Hamlin flopped his hand nervously. "What can anybody do? . . . Have you fired Flood yet? Where is he?"

"I don't know, now," Fent evaded.

"You better get rid of him! The sheriff'll be after him in the mornin'. We don't want him here!"

Crocker's gaze concentrated. "Ain't you goin' to back him up? Against sheepmen, Luke?" His tone was one of surprised remonstrance. "I told you we'd need Flood, an' every other man we've got!"

Old Luke was brusquely impatient: "Back him up? What for? It's an open an' shut case against him! Fontana's likely got word to Sheriff Denton in a hurry!" His ire rose as he spoke. "What can I do? I'd back up 'most anybody but a fool!"

In his exasperated condition, Crocker could do nothing with him. Fent left, going back out the path past his own house, and rounding the corner of the bunkhouse. The glowing pinpoint of a cigarette caught his attention.

"That you, Win?" he queried softly.

The cigarette glow wavered. "Yeah. What you want?" Flood had recognized the precariousness of his position without being told. His restlessness had increased hourly since the shooting of Mateo Madriaga. He regretted now that he had not maintained a strict silence concerning the affair.

Fent came close. "Step over here, away from that door," he muttered. And when Flood followed him: "Win, you'd better pick up your traps an' get ready to dust. Old Luke ain't goin' to back you up."

Flood blustered sulkily: "What the hell! Can't you manage the old fool? You advised me—"

"I know," Crocker cut him off. "Never mind that. Things look different now."

Win threw down his cigarette. "So you're throwin' me down too, eh?" he bit off tensely. "An' where do I get off, I'd like to know! I've strung along with you—!"

"Wait a minute!" Fent was suddenly hard. "I told you I'd side you, an' I'm doin' what I can. Ain't I warnin' you now? . . . You get across the line into Idaho, an' don't waste no time about it! Go to Jeff Aiken's Rafter O outfit, on the Snake. Tell him I said to give you a job. . . . Don't make the mistake of comin' back here, Win! You're all washed up on this range." Crocker's tone was definite. "Now, get goin'!"

Flood grumbled, but there was nothing he could do but obey. He swung away, and the foreman moved out into the ranch yard, listening and alert. Small hoofs clicked and slowed. Fent peered. In another moment he had caught the bridle of Fox's mare. That it was riderless did not surprise him; but that it had got home so soon was another matter. What had become of Race Cullyer and the girl?

Hugging the protection of the sage, Race hid from the unseen horsemen in the night and waited for the first sign of his discovery. What wind there was, was in his favor. He listened to the steady progress of the strange men for several minutes before it died out. At no time did he catch a glimpse of them.

He waited a full ten minutes before he went on, and found time for further gloomy reflections concerning the condition of Fox. She had not stirred since the assassin's slug had struck her down, but her breathing continued. There might still be time if he met with no further delays.

He put the roan to a run now, striking across neutral ground before he reached the Diamond Bar. It was nearly two o'clock when he came in sight of the ranch. Lights blazing in the front of the house attested to the wakefulness there. He was met by the gruff hail of a puncher.

"It's Race—Cullyer!" he called. "Don't stop me! I've got Miss Hamlin—wounded! I must get her in the house!"

He did not pull up until he reached the arched gate of the patio. The sound of his coming had preceded him. An old retainer rushed out.

"Take the horse!" Race snapped at him. He slipped out of the saddle and ran into the patio; and only then he realized how numb his arms had become, stiff and clumsy from the shoulders down.

Old Luke started out of the shadows to intercept him. "What's goin' on here?" he demanded. Then he stopped. "Fox!" he cried hoarsely. "My God—what's happened to her? His fierce old eyes were fixed on the bloody bandage around her head.

"Scalp wound," Race got out. "Get a woman here, Hamlin, quick! And send somebody for the doctor!"

"Take her in on the couch—front room," old Luke pointed, galvanized into bustling activity. "Inez! Yleta!" he roared for the Mexican women.

The stout, stolid *mozas* found Race and Fox in the front room. Having turned the girl over to them, Race turned toward the patio, and, as he entered, heard Hamlin giving feverish directions to the mounted buckaroo at the gate, who was being sent to Paradise for Doctor Barker.

"I want him here damn quick!" the old rancher fumed. "I don't care if you have to kill that hoss an' walk back You hear me?"

The other did. His pony started with a gouging whirl, and thundered away. Old Luke turned back into the patio, suddenly bent and aged, now that he had done all he could. He shot a lowering look at Race as he passed into the house, but appeared not to see him.

Striding up and down the patio, Race waited with sober face and taut nerves. Old Luke did not reappear. Except when one of the Mexicans glided by, the house remained noncommittal, silent. The hours dragged past.

At last Doctor Barker arrived. He strode through the patio with no more than a glance for Race. His steps echoed within, and quiet descended again. Race wiped his face with his bandana.

"Lord! This is the hardest part of all!" he told himself.

The time seemed endless before the doctor and old Luke returned, talking in low tones as they walked to the gate. The sky had paled to the verge of dawn, and their figures stood out against the graying sage beyond. Doctor Barker took his departure.

Race gathered himself together unconsciously as Hamlin turned to face him. He knew what was coming. The softened lassitude in old Luke's iron features told him that Fox's condition was better, but that would not mitigate the weight of the rancher's wrath when he learned what Race must tell him.

Old Luke sank into a handy chair. "Cullyer, tell me what happened," he ordered wearily.

"A ricochet struck Fox," Race responded. "The slug glanced off my saddle horn. That shot was meant for me."

Hamlin's glance darkened. "You was with her before it happened, eh? I thought— Where was you?" he broke off, on a note of sharpness.

"At the Pinnacles," Race answered reluctantly.

The pallor of old Luke's sleepless night only accentuated the thunder of his brow. He jumped up nervously. His big frame seemed to expand.

"My girl at the Pinnacles last night?" he demanded incredulously. "I thought you were at the Dutch John Creek camp!"

Race met his stare unwaveringly.

"I was," he admitted.

"Then how does it come you—" Hamlin's indignation changed to rumbling wrath. "What is this, you're tellin' me?" he jerked out fiercely.

"Father!"

The weak, clear remonstrance startled both men. They swung toward the door to find Fox standing there, pale but resolute, her head-bandage showing white in the growing light of the dawn. She came forward with her accusative gaze fixed on old Luke.

"Mr. Cullyer brought me home at real risk to himself. He saved my life," she reminded gently.

Hamlin sputtered, his features rapidly reddening.

"What are you doin' out here?" he countered testily. "You're in bad shape, an' you belong in bed, girl! . . . This is between me and Cullyer!"

"I shall stay while anything is going on that means so much to me," she retorted stoutly.

He cut her off almost brusquely: "What were you doin' way at the Pinnacles last night? Didn't I tell you to stay home?" In the heat of his ire he wheeled back to Race. "Cullyer, have you been meetin' my daughter out on the range, unknown to me?"

"He has!" Fox answered for Race quickly. "But you needn't blame him for anything that has happened!"

"Fox—!" the old man began thunderously.

Race interposed sharply, a certain amount of impatience in his manner. "Save your bile for me, Hamlin," he snapped. "I can stand it! I guess I'm the one that's over my head now!"

"I should say you was over your head, feller!" the rancher ejaculated, his jowls quivering. "I should think you'd have better sense than to go fannin' off the range to meet my girl a few hours after a sheepman gits himself killed! Didn't you *know* what was goin' on?"

"It happens I did know," Race flashed back;

"no thanks to Crocker—for he never sent word, one way or another!"

Luke was not appeased. "What did you think you four men was out there for, then?" he bellowed. "Was you waitin' for somethin' to hit you? . . . No," he amended, "I ain't arguin' that with you—or Crocker either! He was out on the South Fork tonight—an' back here again, where he belonged! You're a good range hand, Cullyer; I'll give you that. But as a son-in-law, you're out! D'you know what that means?"

"Yes," Race answered slowly, "I know what it means, all right—"

"It means you've got to put a stop to this damned foolishness here and now!" old Luke thundered. "If I'm payin' a man good wages, it's not goin' to be for—"

"Wait a minute!" Race broke in crisply. His face was clean-cut and hard. "You've had your say, and mine will finish the matter. Hamlin, if I don't suit you all the way, I don't suit you at all! I'll just take my time right now. If you'll make out my check, I'll be movin' on!"

"Race!" Fox exclaimed.

"Well, that suits me!" old Luke caught him up belligerently. "I don't need any man that don't need his job!" He turned toward the door to procure his check-book, so agitated that he scarcely knew what he was doing.

"Race!" Fox repeated, stepping forward.

61

Be faced her, shaking his head slowly as he started to go on. "I'm sorry, Fox—for what happened to you," he told her soberly. "I know what you're going to say. . . . It was my fault, letting you go out there."

"But it was as much mine as yours!" she urged importunately. "Please don't go like this! Let me speak to father after he has cooled off—"

He held up a hand. "No, that's finished," he concluded. "Your dad spoke what was on his mind, and I did the same. And maybe he's right anyway. We'll let it stand."

Fox's hand fell to her side. "I—suppose we must," she murmured.

# Chapter VI

## OLD LUKE'S LAST TRICK

The sun was up when Race swung to his pony's back and rode away from the Diamond Bar hacienda that morning.

His heart was heavy, for he had not wanted to leave the double game he perceived beginning on the ranch. He found it the hardest choice of his life as he made his way back to the Dutch John Creek line camp to procure his war-bag and tell Spade McSween what had occurred. There was no pleasure for him in the song of the mockingbird skimming the sage, or the drifting shadow of the hawk that hovered against the blue in the fresh, clear atmosphere.

It was the lifting ears of the roan that first announced to Race the approach of another rider. He looked up. Dark against the rising background of the Cottonwood slopes, a mere dot several miles away, he described a single horseman coming this way. He had no idea who it might be.

As the other drew nearer, however, Race saw that it was Spade McSween. A smile eased the tightness of his lips at this discovery.

Spade's glance was keen as he came up.

"You are all in one piece yet," he said

relievedly. Then perceiving the length of Race's face: "What's eatin' you, Race?"

"You seem to put things together pretty well for a man that don't know," Race countered.

"Well, why not?" Spade came back defensively. "I wasn't goin' to let it slide when you didn't come back! Come daylight, I lit out fer the Pinnacles and had me a look around." He fished in a pocket, and drew forth an empty Winchester shell of standard caliber, which he held out. "That told me it wasn't all clear sailin' fer you, if I needed to know . . . what happened last night?"

"Somebody took a shot at me, and missed. It laid out Fox—wicked gash along the side of her head. I had to hustle her home. She's gettin' along, now."

McSween frowned. "What'd Fent Crocker have to say to that?" He glanced up shrewdly.

Race shook his head. "Crocker didn't show up. Fox told me he was pushin' the boys pretty sharp when she left. Hamlin said he was at the ranch later in the evenin' . . . Fent didn't turn up at the camp?"

"No, he made sure not to."

Race's head came up. "What do you mean by that?"

"Well, read it fer yourself . . . Race, I found tracks where I picked up that empty shell, this mornin'. They hit straight away from there for the Diamond Bar! I know, because I follered 'em before I started out to find you." Spade's eyes were narrowed as he ended.

"Why, that's foolish!" Race responded, impatiently, understanding his meaning perfectly. "Crocker wouldn't have done a thing like that! I tell you that shot was for me. He hadn't any reason to kill me. What would he gain—" He stopped, suddenly appreciating what the foreman would gain in the event of Fox's death.

"That's just it," Spade rejoined, watching him. "What *would* he gain!"

Race was deeply angered.

"Even if it were so, the worst of it is, I can't pin it on him. . . . It's a damn shame!" he burst out hotly. "Spade, I've just played into that man's hands! I had words with Luke Hamlin this mornin', and quit!"

Spade's eyebrows rose. "That does put another face on it," he admitted.

They turned together in the direction of Dutch John Creek. No more was said as they went on toward the line camp. They reached it toward noon, and found Baldy Crebo there alone. Varian had gone out to ride the line.

"Sorry to put you and Stub in this position," Race told Crebo, "but I'm off the job—got done this morning."

"Race, what's goin' on?" Baldy queried.

The ex–straw-boss told him briefly, saying nothing as to his reason for quitting. Crebo made no comment, drawing his own conclusions.

Race and Spade gathered their effects and made ready to leave. McSween turned in the act of mounting to inquire:

"We're goin' back to the ranch, ain't we? . . . Give me a chance to pick up my check?"

"Yes," Race answered.

They were in no hurry, and it was late afternoon before they came in sight of the ranch. Apparently no one was about, but they could not be certain. Race's eyes were mere slits, his face cold, as he and Spade entered the ranch yard.

Bill Denton, the sheriff of Humboldt County, met them at the corner of the bunkhouse. Denton was tall and lean, with deep lines of care in his leathery cheeks.

"Where's Win Flood?" he queried.

"I don't know," Race answered. "Did you ask Crocker?"

"No. I been lookin' for him. Where's he at?"

"Couldn't say," Race responded shortly. "I haven't seen him myself."

Fent rode in while they were talking about him, his eyes inscrutable as they rested on Race. The sheriff accosted him with his persistent demand:

"Where's Win Flood, Crocker?"

"I don't know." The foreman spoke slowly, as though weighing his words.

"You did know!" Denton went on hardily. "You knowed I'd be comin' to see him, too! His blankets an' stuff ain't in the bunkhouse now. . . . Did you send him off some'eres?" he broke off sharply.

"Apparently I didn't have to," Fent rejoined unemotionally. "If he's gone, it's likely he's seen the light, an' skipped."

"Dammit, man!" Denton began; "why didn't you—!"

"Hold on, Denton!" the foreman interposed levelly. "If Win Flood or any other man gets free with his gun, what have I got to do with it?"

"Jest the same, I bet Flood's hittin' for Idaho as fast as he can lick it; an' I bet you know all about it too," the sheriff retorted angrily. "I've got more'n half a mind to foller Flood—there ain't but one way he could go!"

"That'll be all right with me," Crocker told him evenly.

The sheriff studied him warily. "Where's Luke Hamlin—up to the house?" he queried abruptly.

"No," Crocker's broad face was devoid of expression. "He started out about ten o'clock to see some other ranchers. He ain't come back yet."

Denton was about to put another question when he was interrupted in an unexpected manner. Hearing the harsh grate of wheels, the four men glanced toward the drive leading in from the Paradise road.

The approaching buckboard held but one

occupant—Luke Hamlin. He was coming back early; and as the horses trotted steadily on past the house and into the yard without a pause, there was something in old Luke's posture that held the observers. He sat straight in the seat, but his head sagged oddly, the belligerent Hamlin jaw protruding.

It was Fent Crocker who sprang forward with a sudden jarring intimation of the truth.

"Here's somethin' for you to worry about, Denton!" he ejaculated. "You're right on the ground this time!"

As the silenced men gathered around the buckboard, each reacted in his own way to the stunning discovery that met his eyes. Luke Hamlin had been shot. The staring blankness of his gaze; his immobility; the spreading stain on his vest, told the ghastly story.

# Chapter VII

## READY TO RIDE

"Wal!" Sheriff Denton exclaimed as he stared at old Luke's corpse, upright in the seat of the buckboard. He swung back to the Diamond Bar foreman. "Where'd you say Hamlin was startin' for, this mornin'?" he pressed on severely. After his first unguarded cry, Fent Crocker had subsided. He sent a malignant look at Race Cullyer before he answered.

"Luke said he'd see the Blisses, at the Bull's Head; then Hank Rankin, on the Fryin' Pan— Stevens, an' one or two others." If Crocker had been careful of his speech before, he was doubly so now.

"That's coverin' a lot of territory," Denton remarked gruffly. "Hamlin ain't been dead long." He reached out and grasped the rancher's hand. "He's warm yet. That means he got it not more'n two or three miles from here."

"No," Crocker agreed slowly, conscious of Race's gaze on his face. "He didn't have time for many calls. Prob'ly the Bull's Head an' then over to the Fryin' Pan. The other outfits lay over here to the east."

"We better get Hamlin in the house," Spade

69

McSween broke his silence at last. "Miss Fox's got to be told too." He looked significantly at Race.

The latter showed reluctance. "No, I can't do it—"

"She's got to know," Spade insisted.

Race read the faces of the other men. It came to him that none of them relished the duty any more than himself. "All right," he said slowly. "I'll tell her." He started for the house.

He was going up the path when Fox appeared in the door. There was an alert look in her face as she came toward him.

"What is it?" she demanded. "Something is wrong. Is father hurt?"

Unconsciously he put out a hand to stop her.

"Fox," he began; "you must be strong—"

"Tell me!" she commanded, searching his face. Dread was dawning in her eyes.

"Your father," he assented gently.

Suddenly her breath caught. She was staring over his shoulder, the blood draining away from her cheeks. "Father!" she cried. "Is he—dead?"

"Steady, Fox!"

The men had taken old Luke from the buckboard, and were carrying him in. The girl saw his tousled hair; the slack bulk; one of his sagging arms. The truth struck at her. She swayed. Race supported her, as the others came forward.

The impact of the blow to Fox seemed inward.

She was like a marble statue as he steadied her. "All right," she whispered after a moment.

"Can you—manage, Fox?"

"Yes."

He took away his arm, but followed her as she turned to the door behind Crocker, Sheriff Denton and Spade.

Old Luke was taken into his office and laid on the couch there. The four men turned their backs as Fox bent over the inanimate form. Her grief was silent. After some moments she straightened.

"Who did it?" she demanded. The fine spirit of the girl was coming to the fore now.

"I reckon it was sheepmen," Spade McSween put in gruffly. The sheriff looked at him, but did not speak.

"Not much doubt about it," Fent Crocker, inserted tonelessly. "Luke was on business that concerned them."

Race tested the quality of the foreman's voice. If he had been surprised at Spade's volunteered opinion, he was still more so at the feeling which came to him now that Crocker was right.

"Wal—" Bill Denton temporized, listening and watching. The lines in his face had deepened.

"It was sheepmen," Spade repeated. "Looks to me like you could figure this out on paper, it's so plain. Hamlin was seein' other cattlemen about this sheep situation. Crocker says he must've been comin' back from the Fryin' Pan when it

71

happened. Don't that road curve round the base of the Rock Buttes? What'd be easier—"

"That's something like," Crocker broke in more strongly. "Some Basque up there in the hollows of the rocks, with a rifle—he could do it mighty easy!"

He was congratulating himself gingerly, now that the conviction of reprisal by the sheepmen seemed to gain ground. He had not dared give himself over to these feelings until the present moment. Of all men, he stood to gain the most by Hamlin's death.

Fent had wanted to throw suspicion on Race Cullyer on the spot. It had not escaped his notice that Race and Spade had arrived at the Diamond Bar just before himself. But in view of his own position, it would leave him open to counter charges of double weight. Given the easy solution of blaming the Basques, he warily withdrew, a sensation of cold running down his back at the narrowness of the pinch.

"But—do any of you *know* it was the sheep-men?" Fox inquired.

"It hadn't ought to be no turrable task to get an idea," Spade put in. "Them buttes on the Fryin' Pan road are soon looked at!"

"Yes, and I'm going to be out there in short order!" Crocker rejoined virtuously, his face ugly. "If there's any tracks there—"

"Wait a minute, now!" Sheriff Denton growled.

"I know what you'll do if you find anythin' out there you don't like the looks of!"

"What would you do, in our place?" Crocker braced him flatly.

"Wal, in that case," Denton countered grumpily, "I'll jest change my plans an' go too."

While he and Crocker continued to argue, Fox looked her unspoken question at Race. Understanding her, he inclined his head.

"Spade and I will go along," he murmured. "It's the least I can do for you before I leave."

"But—surely you won't leave now?" she implored, moving closer.

Race hesitated. "I can't work for Crocker," he told her.

"But this is important. Please—for my sake, Race? I don't want you to go," she pleaded.

"But I—"

Gazing into her eyes he read there an appeal greater than the one she voiced. "All right," he agreed reluctantly, glad that he would at least remain near her. "Spade too?"

She thanked him with her eyes. "Spade too," she echoed. "I will be glad to have you both continue to work for me."

Fent Crocker, engaged with the sheriff, had not heard what had gone before; he caught her last words, however, as she had meant he should.

The foreman was inwardly furious. "Shinin' up to her at a time like this!" he told himself bitterly.

73

"Damn that hombre, anyway!" On the surface he was his usual cold self.

"Well, let's get goin'," he said brusquely, shooting a glance of intense dislike at Race as he moved toward the door. Resolute of face, ready for whatever might come, Spade was close behind him.

With sympathy in his heart for the girl they were leaving behind them, Race turned to follow the sheriff out of the office. In the ranch yard, Crocker, Denton and Spade were already mounted, waiting for him.

"Make it snappy, Cullyer, if you're goin' with us!" the foreman growled, swinging his pony.

"I'll be right on your tail, Crocker," Race retorted. He did not care what Fent made of his double meaning, as he swung into the saddle. He had no doubt Crocker got it, for the other gave him a second slow stare as they started off.

# Chapter VIII

## NICK FONTANA

The rocky buttes on the road to the Frying Pan ranch were not quite three miles from the Diamond Bar. A grimness had settled on the four men who rode thither.

Crocker and Sheriff Denton rode ahead. The latter persisted in his inquiry into Luke Hamlin's affairs, seeking for something that might explain his death. Behind them, Race and Spade studied the foreman's back.

"D'you notice how quick he was to snatch onto Fontana to explain this business?" Spade muttered.

Race shook his head. "Any man would," he replied guardedly. "It looked bad for Crocker."

"Can't see that it looks any worse for him than it does for you," Spade demurred.

"How so?"

"Well, Crocker's game is under cover. Not everybody guesses his interest in Hamlin shovin' off. But it's known that you quarreled with Luke. If Crocker accused you, an' you countered with a tale of his doin's, it wouldn't stick. Folks would yell alibi—or else they'd think it blame hard, which is just as dangerous to you!"

"That's true," Race agreed.

Spade subsided into silence.

On the branch running west from the Paradise road, the Rock Buttes rose against the sky ahead of them; broken, sun-bleached; like crumbling ruins overlooking the trail. It was easier to mount the bluffs behind them than to climb the rugged incline on foot.

No one spoke as they spread out and began to quarter the ground. No tracks except those of wandering cattle, no slightest trace was found, where the assassin might have approached the buttes or ridden away after the fatal shot was fired.

"It was Crocker who put out the suggestion that Hamlin was killed from here," Race found himself thinking. Was it possible the foreman had deliberately misled them?

Observing the man's actions, Race could not decide. Crocker was intent on the hunt, scanning the ground with almost fierce attention. When Race strayed over on land the other had covered, he could not find that Crocker had overlooked anything.

"Wal, we'll have a look in the rocks," Bill Denton decided.

They dismounted and went forward. It was no easy task to clamber down the rough, eroded crevices to the hollows below. There were any number of these, every one of which was admirably adapted to the purpose of dry-gulching. Stunted dwarf-sage clung here and there, making excellent cover if any were needed.

Spade McSween straightened up with a grunt at a point half-way down the shoulder of the second butte. Near him at the time, Race caught the glint of something he held in his gnarled fingers.

"What is it?" he asked, starting forward.

"Used shell," Spade answered.

Attracted to the spot, Sheriff Denton and Crocker looked at the shell closely. There was nothing about it that seemed to aid them. It was new and shiny, and of the same caliber and make, Race noted, as the one Spade had picked up at the Pinnacles.

"I'll jest take that," the sheriff commented. "It may not mean nothin', but—"

"Wait a minute," Race told him. "I'd like a look, Denton, if you don't mind."

Disregarding the curl of Crocker's lips, he took the shell and examined it carefully.

All four men scrutinized the hollow in which the spent shell was found, without result. Race climbed to an adjacent niche.

"Here's where he was," he called presently. "His ejector threw the shell down there."

They went up. Race pointed out where a scuffling toe had kicked loose the soil at the root of a starved sagebush. There was nothing else,

77

despite Crocker's firm determination to make the rocks give up their secret.

"That closes us out," Fent muttered in a dead voice. The others saw in his face that he was far from satisfied.

"What makes you so shore Fontana had a hand in this?" the sheriff demanded.

Fent showed impatience. "I ain't sure," he retorted; "but, Denton, you got eyes. How does it look? You think I'm coverin' Win Flood when I say the boscos tried to fix him, an' missed. All the same, it got under their skins deep! . . . Hamlin's killin' is the answer."

Crocker's argument decided the sheriff. "We'll ride over an' see Fontana," he said.

Fent looked at Race and Spade. "If you an' I go over there—" he began, speaking to Denton.

"We'll all go," Race put in quietly.

The sheriff did not demur. No more was said as they climbed back to the horses, but Race was aware of Crocker's contemptuous stare as they set off.

It was five o'clock when the little cavalcade left the buttes. The sun hung low in the sky when they left the road and turned in to Fontana's tumble-down ranch an hour and a half later.

Nick Fontana was completely devoid of the more obvious vanities of rich men. Cousin, uncle or grandfather to half the Basques in the country, he was secure in his power as he was.

At first glance his weathered shack would never be taken for the home of a wealthy person. No attention had been spent on its appearance since its construction. Broken panes in the windows were carelessly stuffed with burlap. The yard was littered with refuse.

Nick himself came to the door, busy with a whittled toothpick.

"Evening, sheriff," he greeted. No flicker crossed his round olive face as his black eyes took in the three stockmen. He knew Crocker, and nodded to him shortly.

Fontana was fifty or over, stout and suave. Although his clothes were no improvement over his surroundings, he wore a bland manner of success that effectually concealed his thoughts.

Denton eased himself out of the saddle and studied the other gravely. "Luke Hamlin's jest been shot. What do you know about it, Nick?"

Fontana's black brows went up. "Luke Hamlin? . . . Not seriously, I hope?" he exclaimed.

"Hamlin's dead," Fent Crocker broke in flatly.

"Dead! *Madre de Dios*, that's bad!" Nick's startled gaze traveled from one to another. His simulation of groping thought, although he had seen the light in a flash, was convincing. "And so, you come here. . . ."

"Don't stall, Fontana!" Crocker put in again sharply. "Who did you put up to this job?" His tone was murderous.

Nick's black eyes were opened wide. "I! I 'put up' nobody!" he denied stoutly. "I know nothing about it." He did not lose his manner of friendly protest.

Bill Denton went on to question him methodically. Fontana refused to take offence. His curiosity concerning the circumstances of the killing, at least, was sincere—and shrewd, Race decided, studying the Basque.

It was plain that the task of getting information out of Fontana would not be easy. The sheriff got nowhere with him. Already the man had brought Denton down to a moderated attitude. In the midst of the latter's temperate querying, Fent Crocker determined to bring matters to a crisis.

"We ain't here to listen to a pack of alibis, Fontana!" he burst out harshly. "We know Luke was shot because one of his boys had to knock off a bosco honin' for trouble! Now, which one of your men did the trick?"

No flicker crossed Nick's placid features at the voicing of the deadly epithet. He had been called a bosco before and had survived, regardless of whether the other man later met with a mysterious accident or not.

"To that I have nothing to say," he answered smoothly. "There have been no reprisals, as you suggest. I get along with everybody. . . . If one of your punchers shoots a herder, that is a matter for Sheriff Denton. I have nothing to do with it."

His unperturbed defense was impregnable. Fent, rasped and ugly, would not relinquish the attack:

"It's no secret how you get along with everybody!" he flung back scathingly. "But I know what's goin' on in the back of your mind! How do I know some herder won't come sneakin' over to the Diamond Bar in a night or so an' set fire to our hay?"

"Oh, no, my friend," Nick told him tolerantly. "If you have any such regrettable misfortune, it will not be on my account." He shook his head. "I'd be the last one to do anything of that kind. I happen to own a first mortgage on the Diamond Bar—I have every reason to wish for the protection of my investment."

"Mortgage!" Crocker ejaculated, taken aback. "Where in hell'd you get hold of a mortgage on Hamlin's property?"

Nick's understanding of his surprise was almost sympathetic. "Why, at the bank in Winnemucca I bought it several months ago."

Race's interest at this revelation, swung away from the Basque; back to the girl who waited trustingly at the Diamond Bar. Clearly there was nothing further to be got from the wily sheepman. But for Fox Hamlin there was another jar impending, one she could not possibly be spared. When a sheepman bought mortgages on a cattle ranch, legitimate though the transaction was, there could be but one interpretation of the motive.

"Well, I'll be damned," Spade McSween muttered.

Little more was said. Crocker fumed. Sheriff Denton stared at him inscrutably. Both were stumped, and they recognized it. With Nick Fontana's repeated regrets in their ears, the four men turned their horses and rode away.

# Chapter IX

## FOX HAMLIN DECIDES

The day of Luke Hamlin's funeral dawned clear and windy. Fox spent the morning disconsolate in the strangely empty house, and felt worn out as the hour drew near when she must take her last look at her father's face.

The funeral was set for the early afternoon. Long before that time the buggies began to put in an appearance. Scores of friends from far and wide came to pay their final respects to the dead cattleman.

Fox accepted the condolences of ranchers and their wives with pale-faced restraint. She found no significance worthy of resentment in the unobtrusive presence of Nick Fontana.

Dust whipped up from the desert road as the cortege moved to the little cemetery at Paradise. It swirled under the blaze of sunshine as old Luke was lowered to his last resting place.

The minister led Fox considerately back to the buggy driven by Fent Crocker. The ride home was silent and uncomfortable on the foreman's part. He could find no sincere words of sympathy for her, and was only embarrassed.

It was Race Cullyer who helped Fox out of the

buggy at the Diamond Bar. She glanced at him gravely, sensing the unspoken sympathy in his manner.

"I am glad you were here. . . ." she told him. "May I ask you to come up to the house this evening, please? I wish to talk with you."

"Certainly," he assented.

It was dusk before he turned in the direction of the house. Walking up the path, he was accosted from the shadowed doorway of the foreman's house by Crocker himself:

"Is that you, Cullyer?"

"Yes."

"What are you doin' up here?" Fent went on, insolently. "Your place is in the bunkhouse, mister!"

Race's pause was only momentary. "My place is where I choose to go, Crocker!" he retorted sharply.

Fent's audible snort was one of hatred and indignation.

Race found Fox in the living room, where a fire snapped in the fireplace. She looked small and bewildered in the dusky immensity of the room, despite her manner of familiarity amidst the magnificent appointments of comfort with which old Luke had provided her.

She lit a lamp on his arrival.

"Sit down, Race," she said in a practical voice.

Seating himself, he tried his best to keep the

strong compassion out of his words when he spoke. Nevertheless he found himself comforting her before they had talked for five minutes. Fox appeared to be touched, if scarcely cheered.

"I meant what I said, Race, when I asked you to stay on," she assured him earnestly. "I know what people will think, when I remain here by myself; but I have Inez and Yleta, and I do not care. . . . I know how you feel about Mr. Crocker too, but I cannot help feeling that I need you both now."

"Of course!" he put in hastily. "I wouldn't think of going, since you asked me to stay. But this big ranch, Fox—are you sure that you can manage it?"

"I shall manage it," she said resolutely. He knew from her tone that she would do as she said.

"I admire your attitude," he told her warmly. "But there is more to it than that. . . . Have you found time to look into the financial condition of the ranch?"

"No-no," Fox admitted. "But I suppose it to be all right. Father—"

He quickly shunted her away from the unfortunate reminder of her father. "It just happens that something turned up the other day in the nature of an unpleasant surprise," he put in. He told her about the mortgage on the ranch, the possession of which Nick Fontana had so calmly announced.

Fox listened closely, caught by the tone of his

voice. "What does that mean?" she asked, when he had finished.

"Well, Fontana is a sheepman," he reminded. "He wants land, as he has always wanted it; and he is making money. The Diamond Bar adjoins his range. His object in purchasing the mortgage on the ranch is in the hope that he may some day possess it, banish the cattle, and run sheep from Spanish Creek, on his east, clear up into the Cottonwoods."

"Go on," Fox prompted, as he gazed at her.

"There isn't much more to it," he resumed. "Fontana's threat to you lies largely in the future. You have nothing to worry about as long as you understand the terms of the contest."

"I understand," she replied, her eyes lighting up for the first time since old Luke had died.

Her questions, once she did begin to grasp the nature of her position, were many. Race drew on his own experience or observation of ranch management for illustrations with which to clarify her mind in relation to the problems she would have to meet.

Fox was firm in her decision to see them through.

Nevertheless he felt that he had not told her all, as he walked back toward the bunkhouse shortly after eleven o'clock, and was hailed a second time by the exasperated foreman.

"You stayed a long while, cowboy!" Crocker

began offensively. "I should think you'd have sense enough to lay off, after the old man is laid away. I can tell you right now, Cullyer, you're barkin' up the wrong tree. I'm the boss of this outfit, I'll have you know, an' I'm goin' to stay boss! . . . There's things about the picture here that you don't savvy, but they're enough to stop you!"

Race listened with mounting contempt.

"For instance?" he demanded shortly.

"I haven't found it necessary to consult you before," Fent snapped back; "an' we won't discuss it now. Get me right, Cullyer! I don't mind you havin' your fun; but if you're goin' to stick around here, keep out of my way!"

"Forget it, Crocker!" Race came back at him scornfully. "I don't envy you, you can tie to that! . . . If you want somethin' to think about, you better figure to tie a blanket to your pony's tail to cover your trail, the next time you take a ride out to the Pinnacles at night, unless you can arrange to go around the long way home!"

Fent rocked back on his heels at the suddenness of the attack.

"I don't know what you're talkin' about, Cullyer!" he jerked out defiantly.

Race was not deceived. "Some day you and I will get together and both explain ourselves, Crocker!" he ended the argument thinly. Turning on his heel, he strode away.

Fent stared after him thunderstruck, his countenance working unseen in the dark.

"You think you're almighty damned clever, mister man!" he raged to himself. "But I'll stop you cold, an' I won't lose no time about it!"

# Chapter X

## FIGHTING TALK

Race found much to occupy his time during the days that followed. As the winter season advanced there was work to be done on the range. Under the unrelenting direction of Fent Crocker the fall beef cut was carried forward with dispatch.

There were miles of draws and foothill thickets which had to be whipped out, and the steers driven back to the open range, where the requisite number of two- and three-year-olds could be cut out and made ready for the drive down the valley and across the waste spaces to the loading chutes on the Western Pacific.

Race had his full share in this grueling work. Spade McSween was usually at his side. Spade had not ceased to watch Fent Crocker with covert suspicion, despite the lull which had apparently fallen in the foreman's campaign of hostilities.

"If I didn't know what's eatin' that man, I'd say he was dotty," he muttered one day, as he and Race rode together to comb out the last fringes of the south fork of Dutch John Creek.

"Crocker's come to a dead stop for the time

being," Race responded lightly. "Fox Hamlin spoiled his game by stickin'."

"He's waitin' for Bill Denton to fasten Hamlin's killin' on somebody before he barges ahead," Spade rejoined. "Don't seem to me like Denton's breakin' his neck to get anywhere's, either."

"Well, Denton's no whirlwind," Race pointed out. "He's slow and steady. . . . Hello!" he broke off, staring ahead.

Spade saw what had attracted him. Neither paid any further attention to the buzzard that flapped out of the dry wash a hundred feet to the fore, as they rode down to gaze into the gully.

In the wash lay three dead yearlings. That they had been shot not long before was evident from the scarcely dried blood which ran from the bullet holes in the forehead of each. The flies were just beginning to collect.

"Circle around and see how things look," Race advised Spade tersely.

While the latter did as he was directed, Race went forward to examine the scene of the outrage.

He was not long in finding the empty cartridges. Once more he was struck as he picked them up, by the discovery that they were identical with other shells which he had recently examined. Race had satisfied himself that the rifle in Fent Crocker's saddle boot was of a make and caliber which would accommodate the shells in question. Did it mean that Crocker had intimate knowledge of all these recent shooting affairs; or had he nothing to do with any of them?

The tracks of a pony led away from the spot toward the south fork of the creek. Spade came riding that way in another moment.

"He got in the creek and covered his trail away," he grunted.

"Look at these," Race interrupted, handing over the shells.

Spade examined them briefly. "Same old story," he observed. "That firin' pin ain't exactly reg'lar. . . . Don't know whether it'd mean anythin' or not." His tone sounded dubious.

Race nodded. "Stick them in your pocket," he said.

Across the creek lay the range of Blaney, the American sheepman whose name he had heard a number of times. What manner of man was he? Race did not know, beyond an occasional view of a large, raw-boned, sullen-faced individual who made no secret of his aversion for cattlemen.

"Look there!" Spade ejaculated suddenly, pointing.

Race jerked his head around. He caught a fleeting glimpse of a man driving a pony at top speed down a draw through Blaney's land, on a course parallel with the range line.

"Come on!" he burst out sharply, setting the spurs to his mount.

The two punchers took the creek at a splashing

run. They thundered after the distant rider, the water flying from the dripping legs of their ponies.

"That may not be the hombre we're after at all, Race!" Spade called out.

Race was grim. "That's right," he admitted freely. "But what do you think?"

Spade did not take long to make up his mind. "I think the same as you do! . . . But, Race, that feller is headin' straight fer town. We better let Crocker know about this 'fore we go too far!"

Race's Stetson was yanked down now, the brim blown back. He did not pull in.

"Crocker can take care of himself," he flung back, "and so can I! I'm goin' to see who this bird is if I have to tail him clear to Golconda!"

The ponies raced over the uneven ground at a break-neck pace. It was not long before they began to draw up on the man ahead. When he struck the level range paralleling the road, they had an uninterrupted view of him, half-a-mile ahead, his body crouched at the neck of his galloping horse.

"We'll never nail him before he gets to cover!" Spade burst out.

The long, irregular fringes of poplars which shaded the village of Paradise rose against the sky nearer and nearer. They were almost there.

Race was staring ahead. The man they pursued thundered over the wooden bridge at the edge of town and entered the street. In another moment he was gone from sight.

Spade began to curse.

"Shut up, and keep goin'!" Race cut him off.

They crossed the bridge at a tearing run, and were among the trees and buildings of Paradise.

At no great distance from the edge of town, the street takes a right-angle turn into the main thoroughfare. They burst around the corner in time to see their quarry slip from his heaving pony, drag a rifle from the saddle-scabbard, and duck into Benavides's saloon.

"I told you we'd run him down!" Race's tone was coolly exultant.

They flung themselves out of the saddle in front of the saloon. Race was in the lead as they stepped in, their keen eyes raking the place. Spade paused at the door, his gaze menacing the half-a-dozen Basques in the saloon.

Race strode forward.

His attention had fallen unerringly on the tall boy standing at the bar with a glass in his hand, and an air of bravado in his manner. Race swung him around sharply.

"Let go of me!" the boy flamed with sudden bitterness, his black eyes glittering. It was Ramon Madriaga.

"What were you doin' on Blaney's range when we saw you?" Race demanded.

The other blinked momentarily before he

decided to answer. "Ridin' to town from my uncle's," he muttered sullenly.

"From where?" Race snapped.

"Fontana's ranch," Madriaga mumbled.

"Where is your rifle?" Race drove on, in a voice that said he meant business.

"I got no rifle," Ramon protested in an injured manner.

Race was on the point of shaking him up sufficiently to refresh his memory, when Spade appeared at his side and nudged him. At the latter's meaning nod, he glanced past the saloon window.

The first person his eye lighted on was Nick Fontana. The stout Basque was in conversation with a tall, raw-boned man whom Race recognized immediately as Blaney. The two nodded together in evident agreement over something. Race's brows drew down.

He did not like the look of the thing, but he found no time to consider it now, swinging back to Madriaga. It was Spade who saw Fontana turn away with a wave of his fat hand, while Blaney came straight to the door of the saloon and stepped in.

"Who did you hand that rifle to, when you slipped in here a minute ago?" Race demanded of Madriaga in forbidding tones.

"What's this here, anyway?" a harsh tone broke in behind them. Blaney pushed forward without regard for Spade McSween's cold stare, his gimlet eyes boring Race's countenance accusatively. "What're you brow-beatin' the boy fer, cowprod?"

Blaney was rangy and coarse, with a lantern jaw and deep lines of potential savagery in his leathery cheeks.

"This is none of your damned business, Blaney!" Race told him directly. "But for your curiosity, we caught this fellow riding away after several of our yearlings were shot!"

"Wal—did you see 'im do it?" the sheepman bawled, with an inordinate assumption of authority.

It was no part of Race's plan to allow Blaney to override him.

"Suppose you let me handle this my own way, Blaney!" he flamed. "—Unless this is your herder?" he broke off thinly.

Blaney hesitated. "No—he's Fontana's."

"Oh! So you sheepmen are stickin' together, eh?"

Blaney exploded wrathfully. "What's it to you if we do, short-horn? Yo're pretty officious— but I guess I'm forgettin' yo're the new boss of the Diamond Bar!" Lashing sarcasm rang in the taunt.

Profound silence fell, during which Race Cullyer's blood went cold. Then came his answer—a smashing blow to the mouth that sent Blaney staggering backward with an unintelligible howl of rage.

Up to this moment the Basques had remained neutral, glowering at the two punchers and muttering amongst themselves. But as Blaney recovered his balance and rushed forward with corded face and neck, and huge, threatening fists, they began a concerted movement designed to put the outcome of the combat beyond doubt. Spade had not taken his eyes from them for an instant. His six-gun was out in a flash, its muzzle roving.

"Stand back there, boscos!" he droned. "Jump—before I bust you!" he jerked out, as one or two hesitated.

With malevolent eyes they obeyed slowly, their hands rising as man after man read the temper of the hard-bitten puncher facing them.

"That's better!" Spade snapped without approval. "Now just see you stay that way!"

His words snapped above the scuffle and thump of the battle between Race and Blaney.

After the sheepman's caustic insult, no more had been said, except for Blaney's choking blasphemy as he rushed to the attack. Race stopped him with a jar, their compact bodies meeting so solidly that the building shook. Then Blaney reeled a second time, going down on one knee.

He snatched for his .45, his visage murderous.

Race kicked the gun out of his fingers, and bore in just as the big man staggered up once more. They exchanged stinging, rocking blows to the face and body.

Of the two, Race had been the coolest from the start; but when the other began to realize that his chances of success depended on more than insensate rage, he became more wary. Slowly his superior weight and length of arm began to tell.

"Lick heem, Blaney!" an unguarded ejaculation arose.

"Steady there!" Spade bit out. "No grand-standin' in this!"

The spectators subsided, moving restlessly.

Suddenly Blaney rushed in with wild, flailing blows with either fist. Race ducked, leaning forward instead of back, and seeming to shrink together. The sheepman's hoarse cry of exultation rang as he closed in. Without warning a battering-ram struck him in the midriff, and a look of agonized surprise sprang to his face. One of his feet came up as he lurched away.

Too late to avoid it, Race received the kick on his chest, and crashed backward, impelled by the force of the blow. His assailant howled and made a cougar-like spring, landing on him with all his weight. Half on his side, Race clutched the other and jerked sidewise violently.

Together they rolled over and over, thumping

the floor. Both were bleeding now from cuts and scratches, but Blaney seemed to be getting the worst of it, despite his look of an experienced rough-and-tumble fighter. Bright crimson gushed from his nose and splattered the front of his shirt. His lips were puffed.

On the floor, Race's quick-thinking tactics began to prove themselves. The combatants stopped rolling with him on top. Although it was no easy matter to remain there, he succeeded in doing it. But one or two crushing blows to the sheepman's jerking head was all he could muster. With an angry growl he staggered up, dragging Blaney with him.

"Stand up and fight!" he bit out.

Blaney came at him, panting, his face a writhing mask—only to crash backward from the force of the jolt that met him. He was on his feet again in a moment, mouthing his rage; but he was beginning to tire now, and his movements were slower.

There was no lessening of his brutal intention as he waded in. Race measured him with an unrelenting eye, and a second clean slug sent Blaney tumbling, his limbs lax.

"Have you had enough, Blaney?" Race demanded.

The sheepman's answer was a mad rush, as though he would crush his enemy by sheer force of weight.

Race changed his method in a flash. Stepping aside, he turned sharply and let loose another chopping swing that caught Blaney under the ear and sent him hurtling. The big, raw-boned frame collided with a table, tipped it in rolling off, and thudded down, to lay still, vanquished.

Race straightened to stare around him with out-thrust jaw and challenging eyes. The Basques gazed back, instinctively cowering from him. Ramon Madriaga had disappeared.

Race noted it. He did not show that it affected him as he picked up his gun, which had fallen out of his holster during the fight, and replaced it. His words were crackling when he spoke:

"That's only a part of what will happen, the next time somebody shoots Diamond Bar stock! Just be sure you remember it!"

"But we didn't—señor—" the muttered protest began.

Race shut it off bitterly: "You know whether you did or not! *But I'm tellin' you,* if it happens again, *you'll* pay!

"Let's get goin'," Race told Spade, when no further protest followed his ultimatum.

Spade took a last inscrutable look at the motionless Blaney, and followed his companion to the door.

"That ought to hold them a while," Spade commented, as they rode home. "But Race, the thing I liked least about this was seein' Fontana in Blaney's company. D'you s'pose Nick knowed we was in that saloon?"

"Our ponies were standin' out there," Race responded dryly.

"Well—I reckon he knowed, all right," Spade answered himself after a moment. "The thing is, whether they were talkin' about us or not?"

They found Crocker and Fox Hamlin together at the gate when they rode up to the ranch.

"What're you two doin' here?" Fent demanded crustily.

Race gave a straightforward account of events, starting with the discovery of the shot yearlings, and ending with the defeat of Blaney.

Crocker began to boil inwardly as the story progressed. "Why didn't you ride back an' tell me about this, Cullyer?" he snapped.

"I told you we had it on the boy, Crocker!" Race began impatiently.

"But, these yearlings," Fox broke in hastily, striving for conciliation. "We can't put up with any more of it. What are we going to do?"

"Well, I'm fer fannin' over there pronto an' clubbin' some sheep!" Spade burst out.

Race silenced him with a glance. And when Fox looked at him expectantly, and Crocker glared, he said quietly: "I'm not the boss, and I don't pretend to be; but if I was, I'd have the boys out riding the line nights."

To the surprise of everyone, however, the foreman spoke levelly:

"That's a swell idea! We'll jest start ridin' the line tonight. . . . It'll either put a stop to this trouble altogether, or get us into one hell of a lot of it!"

Race understood his meaning if Fox did not. He was well aware of the potential dynamite in a number of armed men, riding the range on the lookout for trouble. Nevertheless, he believed it the proper course, and was grimly satisfied.

# Chapter XI

## TURNED DOWN

Fox Hamlin was undaunted by the rapid events which had so completely altered her condition. She was not innocent enough to remain unaware of the forces at work about her. From what direction was a further evidence of malign power to proceed? She did not know, and she consequently weighed each unclassified occurrence with deliberate care.

It was for this reason that she accepted with no outward show of surprise the visit Nick Fontana paid her one afternoon.

She received him in the patio of the Diamond Bar hacienda. Fontana appeared undisturbed by the luxury which stood in sharp contrast to the meanness of his own abode. He accepted a chair opposite her without once breaking off his conventional banalities in a smooth, bland tone.

"I found no opportunity at the funeral to convey to you my sincere regrets for your recent—loss," he rambled on. "Señor Hamlin was a fine—even a great—man."

It seemed incredible that this smooth-spoken man should have wished her father out of the way. Fox let him talk, waiting for him to come to the subject of his visit. When he did reach it, it was not what she had expected.

"Now that you have had time to learn the condition of the Señor's, that is to say, your own, affairs," he went on, "I wonder whether it has been called to your attention that he had taken out a—"

"A mortgage?" Fox completed.

"You understand, then." His assuring smile was natural and easy—almost too much so. "Of course there is a little matter of back interest—"

"Yes?" Fox's gaze on the Basque's face was unperturbed.

"You can readily meet that, I have no doubt?" he inquired. "Understand," he added hastily, "I have had no thought of pressing you in the slightest—"

"Why, certainly," Fox bluffed as coolly as he had done. "I was simply not aware of it. It will be taken care of at once. . . ."

"Speak no more of it!" Nick told her with quick repentance. He was secretly surprised that she could meet the interest. Behind his black eyes and his inscrutable good-nature he admired her courage, despite the cynicism of his breeding and experience.

They discussed the condition of the ranch for some minutes. Fox professed herself entirely pleased with it. Fontana never stepped over the modesty of unpresuming interest.

"I expect you will be leaving us before long, though—bound for San Francisco?" he pushed on casually. "There's nothing to keep you here now. And on the other hand, friends, activity—"

"On the contrary," Fox rejoined; "I have everything to keep me here now."

His dark brows arched. "Yes?"

And when she did not respond, he continued: "It seemed to me that fine as your situation is here, despite your misfortune, you would take refuge in something more—sound, shall I say?"

"I don't believe I understand you," Fox countered.

Fontana was deprecatory. "Well, beef is down—way down," he elucidated, waving a hand. "There's little profit in cattle ranching at present. Very bad, right now, and not much prospects for the future. In fact, I had in mind a little offer I thought would interest you. At least it would have insured your capital. What little I could do to help—" He shrugged.

"Will you tell me what it was?" Fox queried.

"It was of no consequence." He smiled. "I thought I might take the ranch off your hands. . . ."

Fox smiled in return. "It *was* thoughtful of you," she murmured.

Her rejection of the proposal was beyond doubt. Moreover, the consummate adroitness of her reply was a source of astonishment to the sheepman. *"Madre de Dios!* She *is* game!" he breathed.

His further attempts to draw her out were unavailing. Fox remained provocatively calm. Nick touched lightly on the riding of the line between their ranges by armed men, regretting the necessity.

Fox took a firm hand here. "You misunderstand, Mr. Fontana," she told him. "The riding of your line is incidental, in that our entire boundary is being so ridden. It is unavoidable."

"But the unfortunate necessity—it *is* rather uncomplimentary, isn't it?" he smiled frankly.

"Not at all," Fox countered. "There are no suspicions whatever as a result of our course. You know the reason for our precautions."

Nick Fontana had no sooner taken his leave than Fox sent Inez, the Mexican *moza*, to request Fent Crocker to come to her. The foreman arrived after half-an-hour's delay.

"Mr. Fontana has just been here to see me," she announced.

Fent's ears pricked up at once. "Fontana?" he grunted. "What's he after?"

His attitude became resentful as she revealed to him the object of the sheepman's call. He went on to cast out feelers about Fontana's conversation. His probing was so apparent that Fox was annoyed.

Fent did not conceal his anger over Fontana's offer to buy the ranch. He pushed past it, however, discussing with her the likelihood of further difficulty from that quarter.

"It's unfortunate—that back interest—comin' at this time," he broke off, a furrow knitting his brow. "Guess you know your father owed me some back salary? I've had it on my mind for some time, but I didn't want to bother you till you knew where you stood."

"No," she said sharply. "I didn't know." He met her look as though defending himself against Hamlin's notorious carelessness in such matters. "How much is it?" she went on.

"A little over nine thousand dollars," he answered.

"Nine thousand dollars!" she ejaculated, shocked.

He took her deep surprise for doubt. "Sure! If you want to see the notes—?"

"I do want to," she said levelly. She had caught herself, after that one staggering moment.

Fent had to get them from his house. On his return, she took the demand notes from his hand and ran through them.

"As I said, it's too bad all this comes at once. I got no intention of pushin' you. Lord knows I'll never help any sheepman, even that way!" But he did not offer to withdraw the notes. "It's come to me two-three times since your father died,

106

that likely you'd be leavin' for the coast before long—"

"This is the second time today that that has been suggested to me," she broke in with a trace of indignation. "What is the meaning of it?"

He stared at her. "Ma'am, I've been boss of the Diamond Bar for years. I've run it, an' I can go right on doin' it. You wouldn't have to be here. But I was thinkin', if you'd take my notes in exchange for an interest in the ranch, then you wouldn't have to worry none. You'd *know* I was lookin' after things."

"But I don't want to do that!" she demurred, taken aback. "I have no intention of leaving. And I am of no mind to break up the ranch, either. . . . No," she took a decisive breath; "we will have to think of something else, Mr. Crocker."

His tone alone revealed his disappointment as he put his next question: "Then what d'you expect to do about the notes?"

"Why, I suppose I shall have to apply for a loan from the bank, if you've got to have the money. I have business in Winnemucca which I must attend to, and I will stop in and see Mr. Brand while I am there. I'll go in the morning."

Fent listened with forced politeness, oblivious of the fact that she was genuinely upset.

"I suppose you'll want Cullyer to drive you in," he said in an expressionless voice. He could not forego this stab at her pride, as he looked her in the eye.

She met his look with one as direct. "Yes," she answered, on an unreadable impulse.

Fent left her without further speech. He was in a savage mood as he returned to the ranch yard.

"She ain't done with me yet," he told himself grimly. "Wait till she finds out how much chance there is of her gettin' a loan from the bank!"

That evening, he accosted Race coolly:

"You'll get the buggy ready in the mornin' to drive Miss Hamlin in to Winnemucca. She wants you to take her." His tone said what he thought of the arrangement.

His eyes narrowing, Race made him repeat it. He made no response, however. Not even Spade McSween knew what was in his mind to make him so silent afterward.

Race was in no better mood on the following morning, as he waited in the buggy for Fox to appear. Not for an hour had he forgotten the gall-bitter taunt of Blaney, the sheepman, in Paradise.

"Good morning!" Fox greeted him as she came out in readiness for the trip.

It was hard to resist her determined cheerfulness. They left at once. Winnemucca was forty-odd miles away, and they could not hope to reach it before evening. If Fox noted Race's preoccupation she gave no heed to it. Long before noon she had won him out of his sobriety.

Race evinced interest in her narrative of the interviews with Fontana and Crocker, and the proposals of each of them. He wasted no time on either, sure he read Fent's object aright.

"He'd give an arm to be able to call the Diamond Bar his own," he summed it up shortly.

Fox was not prepared to go so far. "He takes its problems to heart," she went on to explain her feeling. "I've no doubt he has a certain pride in it. In a way, he has helped to build it up."

"At a substantial salary," Race interposed unfeelingly.

She carried this no further, reflecting that his feeling toward Crocker had been one of long standing; an instinctive antagonism between the pair.

Late in the afternoon they reached a point where the road clung to the shoulder of Winnemucca Mountain, from which an extensive view up the valley of the Humboldt River could be had. For miles the broad desert trough, with the river sparkling down it, molded by mountains and tinted with the clear hues of sunset, lay outspread. It was an inspiring scene.

"The desert is beautiful," Fox mused aloud as she gazed; "beautiful in a way I never appreciated when I was younger. . . . I could never leave this country for good."

"You won't have to," Race told her quietly.

At Winnemucca, Race deposited Fox at the

home of friends, and returned to the Humboldt Hotel.

He was still there, cool and quiet, when Fox completed her business in town the following morning.

They started on the return trip without delay. Race was strongly curious as to the outcome of her endeavors, but it was Fox who broached the subject by remarking that she found business tiresome despite its urgency.

"That sounds as though you hadn't the kind of luck you hoped for," he observed.

"No. It is provoking."

"I take it the bank turned you down, then?"

"Flatly." Fox went on to elaborate her reception at the bank. "What am I to do now?"

"Well," he said at length, "I suggest that you clear the ranch of your foreman's claim at any cost. You must practice a rigid economy, beginning at once. Expenses should be cut to the bone. The Diamond Bar must be made to carry itself."

He spoke soberly, no longer softening his blows; and there was much more of a similar nature to which Fox listened with a growing conviction that he was right.

All the way home they talked it out, finding leak after leak in the present management; small things in themselves, but altogether a steady drain on the ranch. Fox was appalled at the drastic nature of the proposals, but she did not flinch.

She spent the night in the first actual peace she had experienced in days. It was with real serenity that she sent for her foreman on the following morning.

Crocker faced her with veiled gaze.

"I find that I am unable to arrange for assistance from the bank," she told him. "Will you please put the men to work gathering enough cattle to pay off my indebtedness to yourself? We will ship at once."

Crocker's amazement at this announcement was deep.

"Aw—no!" he exclaimed forcefully, "Ma'am— we can't do that! Why, it'll strip the ranch, or near it!"

"I have fully decided," Fox rejoined calmly.

Fent stumbled about nonplussed. "We'll just forget about my notes for the present. I didn't dream of startin' anythin' like this!" He was grasping at straws now as he saw whatever hope he had had of gaining a foothold on the Diamond Bar rapidly slipping from him. His face was a picture of chagrin and conciliation.

"You will do as I say, Mr. Crocker," she replied levelly.

He was too shaken to argue with her.

"—And Mr. Crocker," she added, as he turned violently away, "there are some other things I wish to discuss with you, after you have set the men to work. Will you return later, please?"

Fent did not deign to answer, storming out of the patio like a man affronted.

# Chapter XII

## A DAY LATE

The Diamond Bar buckaroos were none too well pleased to hear that a second substantial beef cut was to be made before the drive south to the loading pens at Winnemucca.

If the foreman was impatient over his task, he did not show it. He had not gotten far beyond his dissatisfying interview with Fox Hamlin before reason asserted itself and he took a firm grasp of his anger. It was a cool, inscrutable man who turned the punchers back to their work that morning.

Several days had passed since the usual fall herd had been made up. The rest of the Diamond Bar stock had drifted back to their widespread haunts in the hills. It meant a repetition of combing the draws and brush patches that was anything but welcome.

The buckaroos hazed together a second bunch of the required number. Crocker's virulent invective, when he laid eyes on it, was unbounded.

"Hell, *no!*" he stormed. "Dammit, what's the matter with you birds? What you got there is the best stock we got on the range! D'you want to run us into the ground? . . . We gotta cut out most of the runs an' culls an' bum stuff in the brand for this drive, an' you might's well get used to the idea!"

The buckaroos swallowed their chagrin, and set to work in earnest, if not without grumbling amongst themselves.

"Blamed if he don't puzzle me aplenty!" Spade McSween muttered to Race. "I had him figured to tear into this bald-headed; an' here it looks now like he was thinkin' about layin' an egg. What's the answer?"

"He's deliberately tryin' to hold us up," Race responded. "We haven't got many days to get our stuff to the chutes. . . . Of course he's takin' his grouch out on us by makin' us work."

Spade nodded his comprehension.

That evening, when the bunches were thrown together once more, the foreman treated them to another outburst of scornful criticism. Still the choice of steers did not suit him, and he wasted none of his opportunity to express himself.

"See here, Crocker!" Race broke in impatiently. "This cut is takin' too long, and you know it! The cars were ordered when Miss Hamlin was in Winnemucca, and they'll be waitin'. You're goin' to meet with trouble when you get there, from the railroad if nobody else!"

Crocker's face was flushed angrily. He resented keenly Race's questioning of his authority.

"Your place on this spread is punchin' cows—
an' I don't mean with your mouth!" he told Race
sharply. "Suppose you just let me take care of the
rest of it!"

"That's all right with me," Race rejoined, his
eyes flashing. "You're told, Crocker. Now you do
what you want!"

Another day passed before the cut had been
augmented to the required size to Crocker's
satisfaction. He gave Race more than enough
to do throughout. The latter did not complain.

On the morning the herd was started over
the waterless desert trail south toward the
railroad corrals, Crocker took care to give Race
and Spade positions at the drag—the hottest,
dirtiest, most arduous task of the drive. Fent
did not relieve them as regularly as might have
been done, either, considering the fact that
most of the steers in the second cut were more
inclined to lag than otherwise, and required
constant prodding after a few hours on the trail
to keep them in motion at all. Helpful punchers
drifted back from time to time voluntarily to
relieve them, but this Crocker discouraged in
various ways, without openly seeming to do
so.

The sun beat down, at mid-day, almost with
the ardor of summer. The dust rose in choking,
golden clouds. The steers bawled and constantly
attempted to break back, until the two punchers

were in a lather of perspiration, their patience worn thin.

"Damn Crocker, anyway!" Spade burst forth at last. "I'd see him in hell before I'd bellyache; but he sure can think up some real deviltry when he tries!"

Race was grim, untiring, his lips set in a thin line. "We can make the riffle here all right," he called back. "This isn't the way he figures to break us!"

Crocker was ahead, querulously cautioning the wing riders to moderate their pace.

"We don't want to run the beef off this stuff before we get to the sand land!" he growled.

The punchers made little rejoinder, muttering to themselves.

"Dang him, he knows what he's doin'!" Slim Browder commented to Hank Leflett. "All the slower the point travels, the slower the drag has got to go; an' Crocker ain't askin' Spade and Race to ease up none. He's figurin' to make them boys haze the whole bunch along!"

The long day dragged by at length. The herd was bedded down on dry ground, to pass a restless night. Race and McSween slept the sleep of the dead. In the morning the steers were pushed ahead once more without loss of time.

If the task of prodding the steers along had been difficult yesterday, it was doubly so today.

They were thirsty and tired, almost impossible to handle.

The shadows were long when the first sight of the Western Pacific yards on the edge of Winnemucca came into view. Little more than the tops of the cars could be seen beyond a distant sage swell, but it cheered the men on. A song or two broke out; one puncher yelled back down the line of the herd.

Race heard it. He knew what it meant, although he could not see anything through the dust.

"We'll be in in half-an-hour, now," he told Spade.

Crocker was in the lead as the point came out on a flat giving a clear view of the railroad yards. Even at that distance it was easy to see the situation that awaited him.

The loading pens were packed with blatting sheep, their wool shining dully in the slanting sunshine despite the dust they managed to kick up in the milling corrals. The siding on which the loading chutes had been built was filled with slatted, double-deck sheep cars. The dusty, dark-skinned Basque herders could be seen prodding the sheep aboard the cars.

"Hell's fire!" Hank Leflett exploded violently. "Our cars 've been pushed up an' we're left plumb out in the cold! It'll take 'em all night to load them blasted sheep!"

The buckaroo stared malevolently, his jaw

jutting. Then after a moment, he added gratingly: "Race was right! Crocker knowed what to expect, an' he jest let it go on! Damn him, anyway! . . . Now we got to water this stock the best way we can, an' bed it down out in the sagebrush!"

# Chapter XIII

## "YOU'RE THE MAN!"

Although he saw his position as clearly as anyone, Fent Crocker took the situation calmly. If he felt resentment at the usurpation of the loading pens by the sheepmen, he did not reveal it openly.

"Bunch the herd, an' hold it here on the flat," he told the buckaroos. "There's nothin' we can do but wait."

"Maybe you'll admit, now, that you stalled too long on gettin' here, Crocker!" Race told him disgustedly. He had come up as the men talked, and wiped his perspiring, dust-covered face while he sat his saddle.

Fent glared at him as though he could kill him.

"You ain't bein' paid a cent, Cullyer, that I know of, for the insinuatin' remarks you've been makin'!" he flung back.

"What d'you think *you* could do right now, that I can't? Them herders've got the corrals, an' there ain't a thing we can say. You might's well make your mind up to it, along with the rest!"

"You can at least go down there and see what's what, can't you?" Race retorted. "You don't have to be so damned philosophical about it! It's no mystery to anybody, let alone me, that you're takin' this thing layin' down!"

Others of the outfit were of the same mind. Fent could not help listening, his face savage. It was not long before he was goaded into riding down to the yard corrals. Race, Hank Leflett, Spade and one or two others went with him.

It was Nick Fontana who had brought his sheep to the shipping pens. Although several cars stood loaded, more than half of his flock remained in the corrals, blatting incessantly, their sharp hoofs chopping the soil to white, billowing dust; the familiar and detestable, acrid bitterness of their odor permeating the atmosphere.

Fontana climbed down from the fence to meet the stockman.

"I see you've taken possession of the corrals," Crocker said gruffly, reining his pony in; "but Fontana, our cars were here first, an' here we are. Is there any chance of you givin' us a break with our steers?"

Race cursed in his throat at the weakness of the foreman's demand.

The sheepman's face did not alter its expression in the slightest. Nor did he speak, except briefly, waving a hand at the close-packed sheep inside the corral fence:

"No."

Fent flushed darkly. "My stock's come a long

ways, Fontana! Time's precious to me now—water and feed too!"

"No," Fontana repeated without a flicker—indeed, without the slightest feeling of concern.

It was too much for the listening punchers. "Blast you, Fontana!" Hank Leflett began harshly. He started forward.

Race grabbed him by the arm. "Hold on, Hank!" he admonished. "The man's within his rights, whether we like it or not!"

Fontana stared back at them as though he dared them to take exception to what he proposed doing.

Crocker spread his hands. "That's that. We'd just as well bed down the steers an' take our medicine." He twitched his rein, turning away.

They returned to the Diamond Bar herd silently gazing longingly in the direction of town. Not a man of them but had expected to taste the delights of Winnemucca tonight. It was a sober-faced outfit that ate at the chuck wagon and turned back to the restless stock.

The buckaroos were not prepared to take their situation without a murmur, however. One by one they approached Crocker with their requests, when he returned from his conference with the shipping agent.

"Why, yes," he said heavily. "No reason why you can't go to town for a couple hours."

Half-a-dozen of them had departed blithely

before Race, on the first trick of the night guard, noted what was afoot. Spade observed also.

"Crocker ain't showin' *no* sense atall," the latter commented to Race. "He hadn't ought to let them boys go at a time like this. No good'll come of it. I'm tellin' you!"

Race assented.

It must have been after midnight when he heard several gun-shots echo flatly from the direction of the loading-pens. If there was any doubt in his mind what was going on, a shrill cowboy yell dispelled it.

He jabbed his spurs home so firmly that the pony started with a bound. Through the darkness he raced toward the railroad yards, the sage thrashing at his chaps.

Half-a-mile separated the bedding ground from the corrals. Race covered it in short order.

At the dark corrals and cars, excited yelling sounded, punctuated by gun-fire. As he drew near, Race's horse stumbled and almost fell over an escaped sheep. Others added their cries of terror to the uproar.

He saw the shadowed, plunging form of a cow pony at one of the corral gates. Behind it, on foot, a gesticulating herder shrieked maledictions. Then sharply, at the dull sound of a blow, the herder crumpled. To the accompaniment of curses, the gate was flung open and a flood of sheep were let out into the sage. The buckaroo rode into them recklessly, his gun banging.

Race was at the other's side in an instant.

"Hank!" he cried, recognizing Leflett as he grasped his shoulder roughly. "Damn you—what are you doin'?"

"*Yea-a!*" Leflett howled. "Let the tail go with the hide! . . . Leggo m'arm, Cullyer! What th' hell—"

Race shook him violently, wresting his gun from him. "Blast you, you're drunk!"

The infuriated cries of the herders doubled in violence, and the vicious spang of a rifle rang out. The hoarse defiance of the punchers reechoed.

Race gave Leflett a violent thrust, and wheeled his pony.

He knew that the punchers were absolutely in the wrong; that the law was all on the side of the sheepmen here. "I'll never stop these boys in time! . . . Why didn't Spade get down here with me?"

It appeared that Spade was before him at this new disturbance. The club-footed puncher was in the midst of a knot of crazy buckaroos at a second corral gate, bawling at them, jostling them and hindering their vandalism. Race dashed forward to his assistance.

"I keel you!" a herder shrieked, maddened and dangerous. It was Ramon Madriaga. A cowboy kicked his rifle barrel aside, shouting derisive

123

defiance as he did so, his own six-gun crashing and spouting flame into the corral.

"Somebody will be killed here!" the thought seared through Race's brain. He was out of his saddle in a flash, and grappling with Madriaga for possession of the gun. The young Basque had the strength of an infuriated bull.

Race jerked the rifle free. He swung it. Madriaga fell back, mouthing curses in which his fellows joined. Race turned. A crack alongside the head with the rifle barrel served to sober the reckless buckaroo. Spade had succeeded in forestalling the others.

Just as some semblance of order was restored, except for the escaped sheep, and half-a-dozen dead ones, Fent Crocker rode forward with wrathful face.

"What in hell is this?" he roared. He stopped, catching sight of Race with the rifle, and bellowed: "What're you tryin' to start here, Cullyer?"

"You know how this affair started, Crocker!" Race flamed back at him.

"Yes—don't go blamin' it on somebody else!" Spade McSween blurted angrily.

Crocker would have retorted harshly, but he was interrupted by the arrival of the two horsemen who pressed forward authoritatively.

"What's going on here? Whose work is this?" one demanded. His bulk, if not his altered voice, identified him as Nick Fontana.

"Yas, an' talk fast!" his companion snapped.

"Never mind, Blaney!" Fontana cut him off. "I'll handle this!" He swung back.

"Why, the boys got out of hand; an' before I got here to—" Crocker began belligerently.

Fontana exploded with cold fire. "You don't have to tell *me* what happened!" he blazed, recognizing the cattlemen. "I expected this from the minute you got here! . . . By God, I'll plaster you for this! I'll clean you cowmen out of this country if it's the last thing I do! You can take that as a warning!"

The big Basque's herders came forward more boldly on hearing his voice. They gathered around him, gabbling excitedly. He had time to listen to them for only a moment before Race broke in:

"Fontana, your warnin' is no surprise to me! I'd go easy with who you've got it in for, if I were you!"

"You can yell your short-horned head off, but you can't yell away these dead sheep!" Fontana's voice was deep and furious.

"You're the man who saw to it that we found a few dead steers not long ago!" Race charged forcefully, without pause. "You can talk mortgage for protection—but you've been trying to wipe out the Diamond Bar as hard as you know how! I don't put it past you to be the man who put Luke Hamlin out of the way too! You tried the same

125

thing on me! I don't know who you've had doing your dirty work for you—" He turned sharply on young Madriaga; "but I've got a pretty good idea! It was likely *you* that took a pot shot at me that night at the Pinnacles!"

"Lay off that, feller!" Blaney burst out intemperately, his remembrance of his beating at Race's hands still fresh in his memory. "You ain't done with us yet whether you think so or not!"

Ramon Madriaga seemed taken aback by Race's charges. The young Basque turned, and for a moment jabbered with his companions. It was another of the herders who accosted Race contemptuously.

"Why don' you look to home for your troubles, huh? Ask Crocker where he was that night you got shot at! . . . I see *heem* at the Peenacles that night myself!"

Race eyed the fellow sharply. Then he faced Crocker.

"Is that right, Crocker?" he demanded.

The foreman grunted. "How do I know what he seen?"

"Were you at the Pinnacles that night?" Race pinned him down. "You were spreadin' the story you were on the South Fork."

"Sure I was by the Pinnacles," Fent answered after a moment. "You have to go by there to get to the South Fork, don't you?"

"What time were you there?" Race snapped.

126

Crocker thought a moment. "About 'leven, I guess." His opaque stare was inscrutable.

"Did you hear a shot?"

"Sure I did."

Race was losing his calm. "Didn't you think there was anything queer about it?"

"Queer?" Fent's laugh was dry and hard. "Don't know why I should. Wasn't that what we all expected?"

"Why didn't you mention it later?" Race prodded.

"I didn't think there was any point in doin' it!" the foreman growled. "I don't have to answer to you! Don't go off the handle now, Cullyer! I know what you got in your mind! . . . Why should I shoot at you, you damn fool?"

"You've got every reason to—or so you think!" Race countered bitterly "It's right in line with your game—the game you've been playing for weeks! You've been out to get me ever since you decided I was a risk to your object, Crocker—and I know what that object is!"

Race knew the situation was critical; that at any moment the slugs might start flying. But his ire was up. He meant to speak his mind; and while Fent glared at him malevolently he went on with stern force:

"You've had your eye on the Diamond Bar the same as Fontana has! You've tried to fight your way to it, no matter who stood in front of you!

127

And when you found out that wouldn't work, you started another scheme! . . . This is the closest I've come yet to pinning somethin' on you—but by heaven, I'll do it if you don't lay off! You try once more to wreck the ranch, Crocker, and you'll settle with me!"

He turned to the herder who claimed to have seen the foreman at the Pinnacles.

"What were *you* doin' at the Pinnacles that night?" he demanded thinly.

"I was camp near there," the Basque muttered.

"Where was he, Fontana?" Race queried briefly.

"I don't know where all my herders are," Nick snapped back shortly. "Maybe he was there—maybe not!"

Crocker was surprised at this unexpected assistance from an enemy. He flashed a look of covert thanks in the stout sheepman's direction.

"Who in hell is this waddy with all the hard questions?" Blaney now broke in harshly. "I didn't come out here to listen to a lot of gab! Let's clean house with these short-horns—!"

"I guess you won't do nothin' like that!" a new voice broke in upon them.

Sheriff Bill Denton pushed his way to the fore.

"I don't need no explanations of what's goin' on," the latter continued, "when there's a bunch of sheep runnin' loose, an' a few cowmen handy! S'pose you fellers settle yore differences an' call it a night!"

There was no trace here of the deliberate man who had investigated the murder of Luke Hamlin.

"Sher'f," Blaney broke in on him hoarsely, his face angry, "these birds scattered Fontana's sheep an' shot as many of 'em as they could—what are you goin' to do about that?"

The sheriff stopped him with a bellow. "There won't be anythin' doin' here that I don't savvy all the way through!" he warned. "Was anybody hurt?"

"*Si, si!*" Madriaga caught him up. "Salvator Liotard—he was knock on the head! He was hurt bad!"

"Where is he?" Denton demanded.

A herder stepped forward, revealing his swollen crown.

The sheriff snorted: "You'll live. . . . Come on, now! You Diamond Bar fellers *vamos!*"

Fontana interposed gruffly: "And my sheep, Denton? These men scattered several hundred of them. Are they to help recover them for us?" His fierce tone conveyed a threat in the event of a refusal.

The cowboys loudly dissented. "Herd sheep"— "Us? I sh'd say not!"—"Not on yore life, bosco!"

Fent Crocker said nothing, morosely waiting.

"All right!" Sheriff Denton spoke with decision. "They say no, Fontana! I won't chance tryin' to make 'em. . . . Come on! Break away!"

The Diamond Bar punchers turned their ponies and rode away through the night in a group.

# Chapter XIV

## A CLOSED ACCOUNT

For a varying period every year in Paradise Valley, the fall season lags behind the calendar. Despite the steadily cooling nights on the high range, the sudden winds there, and the gradual withering and detachment of the golden aspen leaves, piling in heaps in the depressions and niches, even the southward course of the sun seems stayed for a time. It was this period upon which the Diamond Bar entered at the completion of the fall shipment of beef.

The night riding had perforce ceased at the time of the drive to the railroad, and Fent Crocker had been satisfied to let the matter stand.

One day Fox Hamlin called the foreman into the office.

"Mr. Crocker, I've had something to say to you for several days," she began, "I did mention it; but I suppose you forgot."

Fent did not take the trouble to disabuse her of the idea.

"You struck a key-note when you intimated that so large a cut would tighten things up considerably. It is to meet these altered conditions that I have devised a programme of closer economy. The ranch must be made to carry itself, no matter what the current price of beef may be. Our expenses, for the winter at least, have got to be cut to the bone," she told him impressively, unconsciously using the phrases which Race had employed.

Crocker nodded thoughtfully. He had already gone over this ground many times, and he wanted a free hand.

"Of course all this will mean letting go two or three of the men," she went on.

He nodded stolidly, avoiding her glance. "I've already been thinkin' about that, ma'am," he responded. "If you'll just leave it to me—"

"But I don't want to leave it to anyone," Fox countered. "I must not begin by shirking the details. I know the men well enough to decide who we need the least." She named four men, glancing at him again innocently.

Fent listened without a flicker of his opaque eyes. "All right," he said colorlessly; but secretly he was deeply chagrined. Had it been left to him, Race Cullyer and Spade McSween would have been two of the first to go. Fox had of course named neither of them.

Preparing herself for what she must say next, the girl did not note his hardening at this check.

"Mr. Crocker, I am reluctant to tell you this," she resumed; "but it seems necessary. Now that times are treating us hardly, I must ask you to accept a temporary reduction in salary."

Fent liked this still less.

"I don't see—" he began.

"I know," she cut him off. "I fully appreciate your feelings. The necessity hurts me, as it does you. But Mr. Crocker, you have shared our fortunes. Now I feel you should be willing to share misfortune, since it is unavoidable."

They argued it for some minutes; but when Fox began to mention that of course the necessity for his services had not lessened, he withdrew warily. He had no desire to shake or weaken her belief in that necessity.

The talk drifted back to the theme of economy. "Ma'am, I'm well aware you haven't been cryin' wolf. Now, I've thought of a way to realize somethin' substantial on our alfalfa stubble. In fact, I happened to sound out a man in Paradise about it this mornin' . . ."

"But we will need our stubble for our own stock," Fox interrupted. "We've always used it."

"I know—but look," Fent went on. "It's different this year. We've harvested our usual amount of hay. We can bring the stock in off the range when snow falls an' put it right on the hay. That'll save the stubble for your bank account."

"But what will you do with it?" she queried.

He had interested a man with several hundred head of horses who would be willing to pay substantially for the privilege of grazing the stubble off. Fox inquired at length as to the advisability of this move; but Crocker had taken his cut in salary so quietly that she was convinced of his essential willingness to co-operate. Before they parted, she agreed to the proposition.

A few days later Race Cullyer was surprised to see a large herd of horses grazing on the bottom lands along Broken Axle Creek. The Diamond Bar steers were still out on the range. Likewise, he knew that the four large haystacks of hundreds of tons each were more than enough for their winter needs. Nevertheless his instinct told him that something was wrong.

He lost no time in seeking an opportunity for speech with Fox. It came sooner than he expected. That afternoon he met her at the corrals, and went at once to the subject uppermost in his mind.

"Are you sure you're doing the right thing in selling your alfalfa stubble so early in the season?" he asked.

She met his question easily. "Why, yes! I think it was a splendid opportunity to realize a little money that we would otherwise have lost. Mr. Crocker—"

He needed no more to tell him that Fent had been behind the idea.

"Why?" she broke off, caught by his manner. "What do you fear?"

"I don't fear anything," he denied. "But just

133

the same, suppose you should lose some of your hay? It may go high this winter—double its value even—and if you have to buy more, you'll lose more than you're making on the stubble."

Fox felt that his disapproval was a natural result of his distrust of the foreman.

They discussed it further, but Race saw that she was inclined to side with Crocker in this, and did not try to persuade her differently.

Yet during the days that followed it made him more than usually thoughtful.

Spade noticed it. They were riding toward the Dutch John Creek line camp one day, and hazing back from the boundary the stray steers that had wandered too close to it, when the club-footed puncher sounded out his companion on the matter.

"Fontana's bunch has been at a standstill, lately," he began obliquely. "Mebbe you tellin' 'em where to head in did the trick. I wonder how Crocker sees it."

Race had no interest in the opinions of that individual. "I don't expect he thinks about anything at all outside of himself," he answered.

"Why, he put over a nice deal for Miss Fox on them hosses," Spade reminded.

He swung his pony as he spoke; for they had come across a lone cow, which attempted to elude their notice by taking to the high brush. Spade meant to rout her out before he proceeded.

Race was after him in a moment. "You push on through after her," he directed. "I'll stick to this side and make sure she don't break back."

Spade ploughed through the sage, making for a dense thicket into which the cow had disappeared. She thrashed on ahead when he came close; but after a moment Race noted that Spade had pulled in and was dismounting.

"What did you find?" he called.

McSween did not immediately answer. When he did turn, his face was blank, but his tone held a curious edge.

"Com'ere, Race, an' look at this!" he responded.

Race rode forward. From where he paused he followed Spade's pointing finger with his gaze. He was startled to behold a man's boot and leg protruding from under the sage brush. He thrust the branches aside.

Curled almost in the position of natural sleep, but in a terrible condition, lay the body of a man whom he had difficulty in recognizing as that of Win Flood. He had been dead for days. His six-gun lay at his side. The crusted blood on his clothing and on the withered flesh of his hand, left no doubt as to the manner of his passing.

"He didn't git far, did he?" Spade commented soberly.

"Why—we all believed he was somewhere in Idaho by now!" Race exclaimed. "I even thought

135

Crocker might've had something to do with his getting away so quick!"

He bent forward as he spoke, examining the ground. There appeared to be no marks save those made by the dead man when he had crawled into the thicket. But Race caught a flash of something white beside the body. He rose with it in his hand.

It was the flattened top of a cartridge box, and Race paused as he looked it over. Something had been scrawled on the underside with the aid of a soft-nosed bullet.

"Fontana's crowd—got me, boys," he spelled out. He raised his head sharply to stare at Spade. "Fontana's crowd!"

"Who else would it've been?" Spade demanded softly.

"I know! But this must have happened the night Miss Hamlin was wounded, or early the next morning!" Race discovered. "Fontana swore he hadn't a thing to do with any shooting at that time!"

Spade nodded. "It don't change things; but them herders must've been some s'prised, if they shot one man, to be accused of shootin' at another, when you braced 'em in Winnemucca!"

Race's gaze across the boundless sage was concentrated. "It doesn't change that," he agreed. "But Spade, this sure sums up my thoughts for the past week with considerable point! Now we *know* Fontana has been working against us from the start!"

His jaw tightened as he reflected. "We've got enemies within and without," he asserted. "Fontana is the most dangerous, as I see it. He's been pushin' along an underground campaign in his own way. But maybe we've got the means of putting a short hobble on him right here!" he tapped the cartridge box-top.

# Chapter XV

## DEAD TO RIGHTS

The body of Win Flood was taken to the Diamond Bar, Fent Crocker, pretending great wrath at its having been moved, since it had been done by Race and Spade, disgustedly ordered it carried on to the undertaking parlors in Paradise.

Coroner Heitcamp, on his way to view the remains, came out to the ranch with Sheriff Denton to question the punchers. Trips were made to the spot where Flood had been found; much was said about the affair; and finally the coroner's inquest was called.

"Not that I think much'll come of it," Spade growled. "Heitcamp's jury'll be a bunch of boscos anyhow!"

"Yes," Race concurred; "it looks as though Crocker had thrown away our chance, sending Flood's body to Paradise like he did."

As Race predicted, the inquest was a cut-and-dried affair, despite his and Spade's efforts to bring something forth from it that would be decisive. They were not given an opportunity to testify, beyond the bare narrative of their finding of the body.

Moreover, there was considerable difficulty in

getting any satisfaction out of the Basque herders as to their movements at the probable time of Flood's death. Their understanding was vague; their speech was stumbling; they could not remember.

Fontana himself, like a sinister spider serene and unobtrusive and deadly, at the center of a great web, was not even called upon to appear. The coroner's jury reached a decision that Win Flood met his death by gun-shot wounds, at the hands of a person or persons unknown, and the matter was closed.

The general attention was distracted, a few days later, by the impressive marshaling of clouds in the sky, as evening drew on, for a final storm of the year. Sensitive to the elemental manifestations in a country more than half desert, the buckaroos watched and speculated. It was a subject of conversation in the dining-room at supper time.

"Prob'ly a good old lightnin' storm," Pop Devore averred. "This'll change the season in a hurry. We gen'ally git one 'bout this time of the year. . . . It'll be some cooler in the mornin'."

Race could not be induced to enter the poker game in the bunkhouse later that evening, nor would he remain still, going again and again to the door to scrutinize the heavens.

"What's the matter with you, Race?" Leflett demanded. "Yo're as prowly as an old bear."

"Season's changin' in him too!" Slim Browder observed. "Leave 'im alone, Hank. I know what the willies is, myself. . . . Gimme three cards."

The storm hovered for another hour, and then descended in a rousing bedlam of wind, rain and lightning. For ten minutes it maintained a sharp onslaught, while the buckaroos took cheerful note of the celestial bombardment.

"Man alive, them bolt're cracklin' around here pretty all-fired close!" Browder exclaimed, as a vivid flash lit up the bunkhouse with the clarity of daylight.

"Wal, it'll slack off purty quick," Pop Devore rejoined, shuffling the cards with characteristic calm. "You can't squeeze no thrills out of a storm this late in the season."

It was Spade McSween who stepped out when the deluge lessened for a bridle outfit he remembered to have left hanging on a corral gate. He came hobbling back with ludicrous haste a moment later.

"Lightnin' struck one of the stacks!" he blurted excitedly. "It's plumb ablazin'!"

After a startled instant of consternation, the buckaroos scrambled to their feet and burst from the bunkhouse running, led by Race.

The Diamond Bar hay had been stacked, in four long, slant-topped piles several hundred yards apart, in a small enclosed field beyond the corrals. One of them, in the farthest corner of the lot, containing hundreds of tons of hay, was ablaze. Already the orange-tipped flames leaped forty feet in the air despite the slanting rain which still came down out of the reddened sky.

The fire was on the opposite side of the stack, which apparently was burning from end to end; a black silhouette of the entire stack stood out against the weird illumination. It would be a fearful thing to attempt to check, but the buckaroos did not hesitate.

"Get a bunch of forks—brooms—anything!" Race called. "Maybe we can save it yet—it's only burnin' on one side!"

They were at the stack in a moment, panting from their dash across the lot. The flames could be heard crackling and snapping as they gained headway, the louder sounds merging in a sullen, fluctuating roar. The night was lighted up for rods around with a fearful glare.

"Good God! You can't get near that!" Hank Leflett cried hoarsely. "It'll fry a man in no time!"

"It won't do any good for us to watch it!" McSween retorted. "We got to do somethin'!"

Led by Race, the men made a determined attack on the conflagration.

"Pitch the burnin' hay down from the ends!" Race ordered.

They did what they could, but it took no time to discover that they were too late. Perspiration streamed down their faces, mingling with the rain. The heat of the flames scorched their faces and singed their hair.

Pop Devore fell back after minutes of stubborn fighting to let another take his place.

"What the hell!" the grizzled puncher swore. "You can't git nowhere near that!"

It was true. Thick, pungent smoke billowed forth, at times obscuring the lurid flames, blowing with the wind until it drove the buckaroos back, gasping and choking.

"It's spreadin' too, Race!" Spade called wrathfully. "What in hell makes it eat so fast anyway? . . . You can't do nothin' with it!"

Fent Crocker was on the spot by now, staring into the mounting tongues of fire that licked heavenward.

"Stand away from there!" he bellowed authoritatively. "D'you want to be burned alive? . . . Get back, I say!"

McSween wiped the stinging tears out of his eyes and glared at the foreman suspiciously.

"He sounds like he's damn afraid the hay *won't* burn up!" he muttered angrily to Race.

The latter said nothing, but his jaw was jutting in a manner that suggested the trend of his thoughts.

Crocker was still busy calling a halt to the fire-fighting. Due to the uproar of the heightening conflagration, several of the men had not heard his cries. He dashed forward and dragged them back by force.

Fox Hamlin arrived, wrapped in a rain-coat, a look of consternation in her white face. She did not attempt to go near the fire, stepping aside nervously from time to time as burning embers descended to flicker and hiss out on the wet ground.

Crocker returned to her, portentous of mien, waving his hands as he talked. Race stood beside Spade and gazed glumly at the snarling pyre of Fox's brightest hopes. There could be no doubt that the loss of the hay would be a serious blow for her.

The buckaroos fell back to stand disheveled, their clothes scorched and their hands and faces blackened, watching the huge stack go up in billowing smoke. It was burning on all sides now, a roaring sinister furnace that must have been visible for many miles.

"Damn if I ever seen hay go up so fast!" Spade ejaculated. "Why, Race, that fire spread like it was on oil!"

"Well, rain don't soak into well-stacked hay very far," Race responded slowly; "still, this does look queer—"

"Shore!" Spade rejoined hotly, wiping his dirty face on a tattered sleeve. "You got it, as well as I did! . . . Lightnin' never set that stack aburnin'! Look there—" he went on strongly pointing.

The better to see, they moved forward again, shielding their faces from the heat, and paying no attention to Fent Crocker's warning call.

"See them pools, alongside of the stack?" Spade pointed out. "Burnin' away like mad! That don't look like water!"

Race's half-formed suspicions were confirmed. During the height of the electric storm, someone had slipped out here and set the haystack on fire. It had not escaped Race's attention at the start, that not only had the stack been the one farthest from the ranch buildings, but it had caught fire on the side away from the buildings.

"Fontana's blacklegs done this like as not," Spade muttered, his eyes glinting. "We've been waitin' to see the upshot of that ruckus at Winnemucca. This is prob'ly it!"

"We'll have a look around in the mornin'," Race answered thoughtfuly. "Not that I expect we'll find much." His speech was clipped and dry.

"You goin' to tell Crocker, or the girl?" Spade queried.

The latter's negative was decisive. "I won't tell Crocker a thing till I can nail it down, whether he likes it or not."

He had no further interest in the burning haystack, spectacular as its destruction was. In the wavering light of the flames, he and Spade turned to follow several of the buckaroos whose zeal had exceeded their caution, and who had received minor burns which they were anxious to treat.

Neither Race nor Spade said anything as they plodded back across the sodden lot, their boots sloshing in the mud. The rain had not ceased altogether. It began again, in a sudden brief shower, as they went through the gate giving upon the bunkhouse path.

"Where you goin'?" Spade demanded as his companion started away through the downpour.

Race said nothing, making for the closed-in rear doorway of Crocker's cottage, the nearest shelter.

"You're a cool one," Spade commented as he joined him.

Race was thoughtful as he drew out the makings of a smoke and started to roll a cigarette. His foot struck a wooden-cased can on the porch behind him, and he bent to steady it with an outstretched hand.

Suddenly he gave vent to an exclamation. The paper and tobacco fell from his fingers unnoticed.

"What's goin' on?" Spade queried, peering in the dark.

Race held up the can and sniffed at it. Then he emitted a muffled curse.

"Look here, Spade—smell this!" he directed.

The club-footed puncher complied.

"Well, damn my hide!" he burst out, almost dropping the can in his surprise.

The five-gallon can was empty. It had contained kerosene oil. The lingering odor was pungent and unmistakable.

"Crocker, by God!" Spade ejaculated, in a sepulchral voice. "We got him dead to rights, this time!"

# Chapter XVI

## FACE TO FACE

The discovery that Fent Crocker was responsible for the firing of the haystack rang the man's doom in Race Cullyer's mind with the echoes of a knell.

"What'll you do now?" Spade demanded, as they stood on the foreman's porch and contemplated the facts. "It don't seem as though Crocker'd have the gall to look Miss Hamlin in the face, but he has! She's got to be told what's what. I reckon it's up to you, Race!"

Bitter as he felt toward the foreman, Race hesitated shrewdly at this suggestion.

"I can't do it, Spade," he said at length. "It's true this empty can, and the way that stack burned, are damning. You and I know exactly what happened. But you couldn't convict a man on the kind of evidence Fent's left us."

"I don't know 'bout that," Spade demurred. "Anybody could've seen this comin' from the day he sold that stubble for Miss Hamlin—"

"Anyone *on* to him, yes. But Miss Hamlin's education, fine as it is, didn't include ranch management. She'd call me foolish for connectin' the stack fire with the sold stubble. She already thinks I've got it in for Crocker because I don't like him."

"Well, you better git off this porch, an' away from that oil can, before Crocker smokes *you* out!" Spade countered gruffly. "That's him an' the girl comin' across the lot now."

Race followed him through the drizzle to the bunkhouse, turning over in his mind the course of action he proposed to follow.

The next morning, Fox Hamlin found occasion to use a saddle horse. It fell to Race's lot to catch up her mount and take it to the house for her. Fox met him with a preoccupied smile. It was plain that she had not yet gotten over the blow of the night before.

"I am persuaded that you were not altogether wrong about the stubble, Race," she told him pensively. "It was only by the wildest fluke that one of our stacks should have caught fire—but that does not alter the case. Mr. Crocker thinks we shall be able to get by on the hay we have left."

She swung into the saddle as she finished; and as Race made no rejoinder, she bade him goodby and started away.

For his part, he stared after her as she jogged on her way to visit Sarah Finch, her slim, straight back and the brave carriage of her auburn-coiled head made her appear doubly pathetic to him in the light of her trials, past and to come.

"Mr. Crocker thinks—" he repeated sarcastically to himself, snorting in his indignation. "It goes to show what a reputation will sometimes do for a man," he mused on. "It's got her thinkin' Crocker is a white man!"

As the weeks passed, Race kept a wary eye on the foreman. Although no immediate renewal of the foreman's machinations occurred, Race knew precisely what was taking place.

Fent was allowing the heartless attrition of time to get in its work. With the sale of the alfalfa stubble and the burning of the hay he had set in motion forces of slow, corroding worry that would eat into the girl owner of the Diamond Bar more surely than any resounding catastrophe, and without the chances of discovery entailed in the latter course.

With the arrival of December, winter was fairly upon the land, although as yet no snow had fallen. But the skies were bleak, the winds strong and searching, and the nights occasionally bitter.

The Diamond Bar stock had drifted down out of the hills, and for the most part it stayed near the ranch. Already the steers had been put on the stacked hay. There was hurt in Fox Hamlin's eyes when she gazed at the horses which still grazed on the alfalfa stubble in the bottom lands.

Christmas came. Temperatures dropped steadily. Water in the creeks decreased as the hills were sealed. The stock wore its heaviest and warmest hair, that of the hardy horses standing up thick and shaggy, while the morning sun brought out clouds of steam from the frost-cloaked bodies.

It was at this time that the horses were taken from the bottom lands and sold.

Less than a week later the winter descended in earnest. One night the ground was sere and dry and brown. The next morning it was blanketed with snow, a dazzling expanse several inches deep, and still piling up. The storm continued for two days, and when it cleared away the drifts were there to stay.

Activities came to a stand-still. The short days rolled overhead in dreary procession. The cattle trampled the lands adjacent to the ranch and the creek; hay was thrown down to them, and the stacks steadily diminished. At the same time, the price of hay went up. It had been high late in the fall, as Race had predicted; now it was at a level which would prove prohibitive should Fox find it necessary to procure more.

The cattle were no little trouble to the buckaroos as the winter wore on. Seeking to avoid the winds, they became bogged down in drifts in the depressions. As the temperature at mid-day moderated, a languor struck at them. They had to be tailed-up and hazed into the open; sometimes to be fed from a wagon where they were.

During the early part of March, events began to occur in rapid order.

The first made a considerable impression on Race. Together with Hank Leflett, he had been sent by Fox Hamlin to Paradise, to bring out certain supplies of which the ranch stood in need.

They had done their errands, and were driving out of town, when Leflett pointed out to Race a novel sight. Behind them, two men stepped out of a saloon door, talking earnestly, one with a hand on the other's shoulder which he took down as the punchers watched, as though suddenly conscious of it. They were Nick Fontana and Fent Crocker.

"That's damn queer—seein' them together!" Leflett remarked gruffly. "Mebbe they're buryin' the hatchet."

Race said nothing. He did not forget the incident, however.

A few nights later, a chinook descended, and by morning the snow had disappeared from the face of the range as if by magic. The sun became ardent once more. The creeks, which until now had been mere trickles, suddenly broke their icy bonds and sprang to full-bodied, rushing life.

And none too soon. Fox Hamlin estimated that she had barely enough feed to carry her through, and that only by the most rigid economy.

"It's gettin' 'long about time for Crocker to open them Broken Axle Creek head-gates," Spade commented to Race. "He's got less'n a week, now, before the fifteenth."

The dam to which he referred was a mile above the ranch. It had been the custom for years to open the head-gates and flood the bottom lands before the water-master came on the job on March 15th. This extra water was counted upon to reach portions of the Diamond Bar hay lands which could not be reached by normal irrigation during the summer, and usually were watered by a small stream running down from the Cottonwood summit.

"Yes," Race agreed. "Fent will be at that any day now."

But he did not let it go at that. It was he who next remarked the passage of time, with nothing done about the water.

"Crocker is stallin' again," he told Spade grimly, several days later. "Up to his old tricks. Here it is the fourteenth, and he hasn't even ridden out to the creek yet!"

"Why don't you throw it into him?" Spade demanded. "Make him do somethin'!"

"And tip my own hand? Not yet." Race told Spade what he had seen in Paradise not long before. "I don't see how Fontana and Crocker bein' together can hook up with this," he concluded; "but they're figurin' on something together, and I'm watching like a hawk!"

"Well, that's all right," Spade answered after a thoughtful pause; "but in the meantime, what about the water, Race?"

"I'll see about the water myself," Race promised, his jaw tightening. "I'll ride over there from the North Fork on my way home. If Fent hasn't been there yet—out the head-gates go!"

He arrived at the Broken Axle Creek dam late that afternoon. As he expected, it had not been touched. The water had backed up for half-a-mile, and there was a good head. Race went methodically about kicking the planks out and releasing the flood.

The released waters rushed out in a widening flood and inundated the bottom lands. Race watched it with satisfaction. He knew that it would be observed below, and that Crocker would take exception to what he had done, but he did not care.

As he expected, the foreman was waiting for him when he got back to the ranch. Crocker and Fox Hamlin were talking by the gate when Race rode into the yard, and Fent hailed him forward.

"Has it come to the point where you're takin' matters into your own hands, over my head, Cullyer?" he demanded. "Why didn't you ask me about that water?" His tone was harsh.

"I knew what you'd say, for one thing," Race told him, stifling his leaping anger. "What's the matter with you, Crocker? We've always had that water."

"That don't excuse you a bit!" Fent raged. "Are you boss here, or am I?"

It flicked a raw spot. Race's eyes were dangerous.

"You don't understand, Race," Fox put in, temperately. "Mr. Crocker says—"

"He understands, all right!" Crocker brushed over her masterfully. "He knows Fontana's jest waitin' to get us in trouble—with the watermaster or anybody else he can!"

Ignoring him, Race scanned Fox's face.

"You see how it is," she told him softly.

"I do see," he answered shortly, and would say no more.

Less than a week later, meeting Pop Devore at the Dutch John Creek line camp, Race listened while the grizzled veteran told how he had run across surveyors in the hills above the ranch. Devore had talked with them. They were working for Fontana, laying a line for pipes by which the sheepman expected to bring to his own range the waters of Soapstone Springs, which he owned, but which he had never been able to use before, except for flocks passing through to the Forest Reserve.

"Soapstone Springs!" Race interrupted. "Why, that's water we've been using for the upper alfalfa fields!"

Devore grinned toothlessly: "Shore. Fontana figgers we've used it 'nough, I reckon. Anyhow, he's pipin' it down to his land."

"And that means we won't get that water

154

this summer," Race said slowly. His thoughts, however, were like lightning. "If it hadn't been for my letting down those head-gates, we wouldn't have gotten any water at all for the upper field." His eyes hardened. "That completes the thing! I'm going to go and talk to Miss Hamlin now!"

He lost no time about it. Fox received him at the ranch house that evening with her usual welcoming smile.

"Fox, I've got something to tell you that you won't like," he began.

"What is it, Race?" she asked reasonably.

Without hesitation he put the pieces of his case against Crocker together—how he had seen Fent talking with Nick Fontana; how Fent had stalled on opening the water-gates, knowing its results; and how the information had come that the sheepman was planning to use Soapstone Springs himself this season.

Fox's face was serious when he ended.

"Hank Leflett saw Fontana and Crocker together, as well as I did, Fox," Race ended quietly. "You can ask him, if you—"

She came to a decision abruptly. "I do not doubt you, of course. Only it seems such a rude awakening." She got up and moved toward the door. "Wait here a moment, please. I shall have Mr. Crocker called in."

Fent came in after some delay, his usual blunt

self. He shot a darkening glance at Race.

"Mr. Crocker," Fox began at once, "I presume you have heard what Mr. Fontana proposes to do with the water from Soapstone Springs. That means that we will receive no water from that source for the upper alfalfa field. Will you explain the coincidence at a time when, but for Mr. Cullyer, we should have had no water at all there, even at this time, from Broken Axle Creek?"

Fent was instantly on the defensive. "That was no coincidence!" he growled. "Fontana planned that, damn him! I'll admit I was wrong about the head-gates—"

"Then perhaps you will explain what it was you were talking about with Mr. Fontana in Paradise, a week ago Friday?" Fox thrust on with cool decision.

He stared at her. "I saw him, yes!" he got out after a moment. "We was arguin' about the creek water! He warned me not to use it; and I told him to go to—"

"With your hand on his shoulder?" Race inserted bitingly.

Crocker whirled on him. Face to face they stared their enmity and contempt.

"Damn you, Cullyer You're tryin' to cut the ground out from under me—!"

"That will do, Mr. Crocker!" Fox told him coldly. "I have heard enough to satisfy me

156

that you have been unfaithful to me and to the Diamond Bar! Have you anything to say?"

"You bet I've got somethin' to say!" Fent raged. He swung on Race, his face congested. Fox had never heard such a torrent of invective and abuse as he poured forth now.

"That's enough!" she commanded ringingly. "I asked you whether you can defend yourself against this charge I am making!"

Fent sneered. "I know who's makin' the charges, all right!" He returned to Race, ignoring her question. "I suppose *you'll* be the new boss of the Diamond Bar," he snapped contemptuously.

Race sprang out of his chair as though stung. Fox stopped him with a hand on his arm.

"Wait," she told him calmly. "You *are* the new foreman, from this moment. . . . Mr. Crocker, I must tell you that I have no further use for your services!"

# Chapter XVII

## CROCKER STRIKES

In a drizzling rain Race Cullyer came out of the foreman's cottage licking an envelope and sealing it. Spade McSween gave his cinch a final jerk and straightened, turning. His slicker flopped about his legs as he stood beside the pony.

"You'll do! You didn't even git ink on yore fingers," he grinned, as Race handed him the envelope containing the application for the summer's grazing permits on the Santa Rosa Forest Reserve, which Spade was to mail in Paradise.

He tucked the envelope away. "Race, what are you goin' to do about the upper hay field? There won't be no crop up there this year, with the spring water goin' into Fontana's pipes. This rain'll run off in no time."

"I've got it figured out how to take care of that," Race replied shortly.

"How?" Spade demanded curiously. "You can't bust Fontana's pipe line. That won't do no good."

"No, but I'll put that line out of commission just the same!"

"How'll you do it?" Spade persisted.

"Why, those surveyors laid down a steadily sloping course for the line to follow off the hills. I'll go up and change a few stakes so the pipe will have dips in it." Race's gaze was level. "There's sand in Soapstone Springs, and it shouldn't be many days before those dips begin to fill up. They'll act like traps. When that happens, Mr. Fontana's pipe line is going to cease functioning!"

"My hell!" Spade ejaculated, staring. "You can't do that! Look at the chance you'll be runnin'! It's as much as yore life's worth, monkeyin' with them stakes! Why, Race, you'd be potted before you got your hand loose from the first one of 'em!"

"I'll just take that chance," responded the new foreman of the Diamond Bar.

"No you won't either!" Spade insisted. "Leave it go, Race! Or wait till I c'n go with you anyway!"

"No," Race answered after a moment. "This is somethin' that can't wait. It will be too late when Fontana gets busy laying the pipe. . . . This is just the kind of a day for my work, Spade."

Spade rode away, muttering curses against the letter which took him away from the scene of action at so critical a time.

Half an hour afterward, Race rode away from the Diamond Bar on a fractious but mettlesome roan. He pushed it steadily across the range toward the swelling Cottonwood slopes, keeping out of the way of even his own men.

The drizzle persisted, sifting out of the characterless, leaden sky, just heavy enough to make visibility poor for any distance. From the first bench of the foothills he looked back. Paradise Valley was no more than a misty, curtained void.

Farther on, he came to the edge of the Diamond Bar holdings. Here he drew in the roan to a plod, and kept a close watch ahead. The land he was entering was public domain, wild and rough; but that was no guarantee that herders might not be posted below Fontana's quarter-section, which contained Soapstone Springs.

Race stuck his six-gun into his trousers-band on the left side, ready to hand under the edge of the slicker, and pushed on, expecting at every moment the necessity for meeting a sharp attack; perhaps for making a run for his life.

The silence of the mountain side was profound. There was only the swishing of the brush, flirting the collected rain which had long since soaked his knees; and the sodden plodding of the roan.

He came out on a wide trail, and knew that Soapstone Springs was near. His vigilance redoubled. Getting down, he moved forward on foot, probing the befogged vacancy ahead. Still no sharp challenge arrested him, no rifle flashed in the obscurity.

Leaving his horse behind, he reached the

springs, a rocky depression with an overflow track leading off down the slope. He saw at once why the water had not reached the ranch, although Fontana was not yet using it. A small dam had been constructed, backing up the pool. He noted with considerable satisfaction that the pipe attachment was low in the face of the dam, where sand might readily enter it.

The first stake for the proposed pipe line was near. Race noted its direction. He went back for the roan, and circled around to pick up the line at a point below the springs. Knowing the suspicious nature of the Basques, he did not propose to leave tracks where they could be readily discerned.

For this reason he fastened the roan at a clump of willows in the old course of the overflow and went about his work on foot.

It was no task to find a means of putting a first dip in the line by changing the stakes. After that, Race had to climb and hunt, looking it seemed in vain for what he wanted, every minute expecting to be violently attacked.

He was content with no less than three dips, in case one or another should not work as he expected; for he had dared make none of them so pronounced as to be noticeable. The last change necessitated altering the stakes for more than a quarter-mile. He swore under his breath at the hardness of the soil.

The thump of the rock with which he drove the stakes echoed abroad. Time and again he lifted his head to listen. Was some wily guard watching with the intention of changing the stakes back when he was gone? He decided not. The reaction to his discovery would be sharper than that.

Race finished his task at last and climbed back to the roan.

"Now we'll see what happens!" he murmured as he mounted and turned down the slope.

As time dragged on, and Race waited for results from his stratagem, he found many things to occupy his time. The ranch worked smoothly by virtue of his strict application to his duties, but it did not prevent the men from watching what he did with unfeigned curiosity.

It was at this time that the news came of Fent Crocker's activities. Stub Varian returned from town one day, full of it, and Race and Spade listened to his account.

With the money at his command, Fent had bought into the Lazy A, a small spread to the west of the Diamond Bar, whose owner, Tom Morgan, had recently died. Mrs. Morgan had been glad of a partner who knew so thoroughly the ins and outs of the cattle business.

Fox Hamlin took a generous view of the matter when Race told her about it.

"I am glad to hear that Mr. Crocker has been able to find something to do," she said, "but I am not pleased to learn that he has remained so near us. I had hoped we would see no more of him in Paradise Valley."

Race had not yet told her what he had done about Fontana's pipe line. Moreover there was a bare chance that he had miscalculated about the pipes. Days had passed, and still the old overflow from Soapstone Springs remained dry.

"It will take weeks where I thought it would take days for that line to fill up with sand," Race mused to himself soberly. "No use of my tormentin' Fox with false hopes. She thinks she knows how things stand."

He was jogging along on his way to Paradise as he entertained these thoughts, for he expected the return of the grazing permits any time now.

There was a sheaf of letters in the Diamond Bar box at the Post Office, and Race shuffled them where he stood as he pulled them forth. He found the letter he was looking for. Stepping back out of the building, he tore off the corner of the envelope.

It was something of a shock to find, rather than the expected permits, a remittance covering the amount of the application advances, and a terse letter announcing that the quota for cattle grazing on the Reserve having already been filled, the application of the Diamond Bar ranch must therefore be refused.

A jarring voice broke in on Race's consternation

then. He glanced up to see Fent Crocker in conversation with Rankin, of the Frying Pan.

"Yes," Crocker bragged, "I'm runnin' four-five thousand head up on the Reserve this summer. Feeders. . . . Eh? Sure, I got my permits a week ago. I always get what I go after!" His flinty gaze drifted to Race as he ended, and he noted the look of concern on the other's face. When his eyes dropped to the letter in Race's hand, he understood the situation perfectly.

His dry chuckle was implacable. "Well, Cullyer!" he observed insolently. "It looks like you got left behind this time. But you can always buy hay. . . . Maybe you'll get enough of that job yet, before *you* get done!"

"Crocker, you deliberately tried to cut my throat in this permit business!" Race charged, flushing darkly. "You've known for a long time how many head of cattle can be got up on the Reserve, and you made sure to forestall us!"

Rankin, an elderly rancher with a florid face and drooping mustache, stared at them with raised brows.

"Sure I did!" Crocker admitted meanly.

Race met his truculent gaze without wavering. "You don't know when you're well licked, Crocker," he said distinctly. "It looks like you'll need another dose to finish you!" His face was grim, his jaw hardened.

Crocker blustered loudly: "What're you tryin'

to give me? I got a right to them permits! Damn your gall, where d'you get off, anyway?" His cheeks, his broad forehead, even his throat was dark with pounding blood. His mind hovered near his six-gun.

"You know what I'm driving at!" Race told him levelly. "If you mix into my affairs, you've got to fight!"

Crocker elected to fight on the spot. At the same time that his gun came out of the leather, Race's hand darted forward. A wrench, and Fent yelped with the pain of a twisted wrist. Race threw the .45 into the dust of the street.

"You're too slow, Crocker!" he taunted. "Your hand—your brains—everything about you is too slow! Let me warn you here and now! One of these days something is going to hit you, and you'll think it's a landslide—but it'll be me!"

Crocker stared his defiance, fingering his injured wrist, his face working.

Race eyed him coldly for another moment, and then deliberately turned away.

# Chapter XVIII

## LICKED

"Then we are unable to graze any steers up on the Forest Reserve this summer?" Fox Hamlin said slowly and unbelievingly.

Race gazed at her as she turned back to her father's desk in the little office to hide her momentary agitation. Fresh from Paradise, he had just told her the news contained in the letter refusing their grazing permits.

"Mr. Crocker has taken out his enmity toward us in a remarkably short time," Fox went on in a matter-of-fact tone. She had herself in hand once more.

"It was not sudden," Race shook his head. "It built up over a long period, and this is its natural result." He told her how he believed Crocker's attitude toward her father had altered with time; how the ex-foreman had come to think of the Diamond Bar as his own by some peculiar right of his own conception.

Fox's gaze widened as Race told her how, with Luke Hamlin's death, Crocker had seen his chance at last, and had tried desperately to drive Race away, that she might more readily be disposed of or discouraged. The girl understood now how Fent's offer to accept an interest in the ranch fitted in with this programme.

Her cheeks reddened when she saw, through Race's sober explanation, how Crocker had become angered at his disappointment, and had determined to tear down the ranch. She listened with indignation, but no longer with doubt, to the story of Race's discovery of the empty kerosene can, after the haystack fire.

"His game has been consistent throughout," Race concluded; "but it would be nearly impossible to pin anything on him. Even in the matter of these permits, he is strictly within his bounds. Crocker's betrayal was in taking advantage of his knowledge of your methods."

"I understand that of course," Fox rejoined. "But it leaves us exactly where we were. I am afraid we are whipped. The number of cattle we now have is not enough to carry the ranch. And yet we could not feed more if we had them! I can see no hope in our position."

Her use of the plural pronoun made him realize how stiff the uphill fight would be.

"I haven't altogether given up the upper hay field," he said frankly. "I did what I could about that, but it will be too late for a first crop anyway."

At her look of inquiry, he told her what he had done with the stakes of Fontana's pipe line.

"But wasn't that—wrong?" she faltered.

"I know what you are going to say," he caught her up. "Fontana owns the springs. But why, except that he may use them against us in this manner? This is no case of right or wrong! It is a fight, and it means win or lose!"

Fox's eyes brightened, but she remained perplexed.

"Then what do you propose doing?" she asked.

Race remained silent for some moments. "I should like to run sheep," he said at length.

She stared at him blankly.

"Sheep! Why, that's—impossible!" she exclaimed, provoked. "This is a cattle ranch. I will not change that!"

"There will be no necessity for changing it."

"But, Race!" she insisted, puzzled. "We know absolutely nothing about sheep!"

"No," he admitted levelly; "but anyone may learn. . . . Now, look here." He sat forward. "We've got to do something! You've seen Fontana's hand. He's making money—buying mortgages! What is to prevent us from fighting fire with fire—making money the same way the sheepmen do?"

"How will you go about it?" Fox protested strongly. "With little hay, we will need all our second-grade range as it is."

"There's the Reserve," Race answered surprisingly. "What is the matter with filing permits to graze sheep on the Reserve, and taking a

168

chance of beating Fontana out? He has never had any competition there—maybe we can catch him asleep!"

Fox was a prey to excitement now. She was not far behind him in fighting spirits.

"Then what?" she prompted. "To get permits, you must put up the grazing fees. We could meet that; but we cannot buy sheep. I can get nothing from the bank, of course. It would mean failure to have the permits, and be unable to procure the sheep."

"Leave that to me," he replied, knitting his brows.

"If we can get the permits, we'll have an ace in the hole. I'll promise to do the rest."

She leaned back in the swivel chair.

"I *will* depend on you," she accepted at once.

No less confident than herself, though his plan was not what Fox thought it was, Race was nevertheless chary of announcing his course to anyone else while he waited for the grazing permit applications to be answered. A day or two later, something happened which turned his thoughts into another channel.

He and Spade were riding across the range toward the east boundary, and they had just examined the Soapstone Springs overflow again without encouragement, when Spade called attention to the slow coalescing and massing of clouds in the sky.

"We'll get somethin' outa that if I don't miss my guess," the club-footed puncher commented, squinting keenly.

The storm fell with surprising suddenness, looming overhead and shadowing the land.

"Come on over to Piute Rock!" Race called, as the wind swooped, and the cold rain rattled like shot. "This'll be over in half-an-hour!"

Their ponies scampered through the sage. In five minutes they arrived at the rocky butte overlooking Piute Meadows, and made their way to the overhang cave in the side of the great rock.

"Somebody musta been expectin' us!" Spade remarked as he swung out of the saddle. He indicated a pile of dead brush, arranged in the mouth of the cave as though in preparation for a fire.

Race glanced around. "Might's well touch that off while we're here," he answered.

He knelt, cupping his hands as he struck a match. The small blaze leapt up, reflecting on the rocks. In the open, the rain slanted down sharply.

"Good thing you thought of this place," Spade said, looking it over with curiosity. "I git rheumatism somethin' awful in my foot when I git wet."

"Got to favor anything like that," Race responded. "Did you ever—" He broke off, attracted by his companion's manner.

Spade's six-gun came out in a flash. His face

was sharp as he peered into the depths of the rocky cavity.

"Somebody's hidin' back in there," he snapped. "I seen the light glint on somethin'. . . . Come on out, you!"

For a moment there was no answer to his command. Then a form detached itself from the shadows and came forward. A white face stared, to resolve into the sullen features of Ramon Madriaga, the Basque herder. A rifle slanted in his grasp.

"You again!" Spade barked pugnaciously. "Drop that gun, bosco, before I drill you through the belt!"

Madriaga complied, watching the .45 trained on his middle.

"What're you doin' here on our range?" Spade demanded harshly.

"I was going from Fontana's upper camp down to the Burnt Creek camp," the Basque muttered. "The rain caught me—I come here, same as you."

"What was you hidin' back in there for then?" Spade pressed on. "Speak up!" he bit out, taking a step forward as the other hesitated.

"I know you don't like me," Ramon answered bitterly. "I theenk I hide till you are gone."

"So we don't like you, eh?" Spade ground out. "And you don't like us either—is that it?" His tone hardened. "You wasn't figurin' to pot us, back in there, was you?"

Madriaga only stared his defiance.

"Why don't you say somethin'?" Spade prodded, giving him a bang alongside the head. "Damned bosco sidewinder!"

"Leave off, Spade!" Race demurred soberly. "He's probably telling the truth for once."

"He shot our steers, didn't he?" Spade raged. "Ever' time we ride out here near our boundary, we fall over him!" He swung on Madriaga. "What are you, anyway—a herder, or Fontana's gunman?"

"I tell you what I do." Ramon's retort was barely audible, but his stare was implacable.

"Don't talk back to me!" Spade jerked out, giving him another bang. "Like as not you're the hombre that did fer Win Flood! It was yore old man that Flood killed, wasn't it? I wouldn't put it past you to be the bird that knocked off Luke Hamlin too! . . . What'll we do with him, Race?" His manner said that he required only the other's sanction to put his own ideas into effect.

"What *can* you do with him?" Race demanded impatiently.

"You don't think he's our man, do you?" Spade queried. "Take a look at his rifle anyway. What caliber is it?"

Race picked it up, studying Madriaga as he did so. "It's a .30-30," he announced.

"Yeah? Same as the shells we been lookin' at so much lately," Spade averred accusatively.

"That may not mean a thing," Race pointed out.

"No? Well, maybe it does!" Spade swung on the Basque. "D'you know anything about Hamlin gettin' shot?" he demanded fiercely.

"No! No! I know notheeng!" Ramon exclaimed.

Spade grunted. "You don't know nothin' about anything, do you? . . . Where's yore hoss?" he broke off shortly.

"I haven't got any horse."

"No hoss, eh?" Spade would have framed another question, but Race stopped him:

"You won't get anything out of him."

"Mebbe not," Spade growled. "But I'll bust him the next time I catch him on Diamond Bar land!"

Something furtive leaped to Madriaga's face for the first time as he glanced at Race. Perhaps it was hope.

Race faced the herder sternly. "Don't you make any mistake, Madriaga! This is the second time we've nailed you. Don't let us catch you on our range again, or you'll have a different story to take back to Fontana—if you get there at all!"

Madriaga indicated that he understood.

"Well, then, git!" Spade exploded disgustedly, his face red. "If you stay in my sight much longer, I'll take a crack at you anyway!"

Madriaga started for the open. He hesitated. "My—rifle?" he queried.

Taking the Winchester, Spade angrily broke it

with a smashing blow against the rocks. "Here—
take it!" he snapped, flinging it down.

The Basque's face knotted with hatred and
bafflement. Then he darted out into the subsiding
drizzle and made off.

"We better follow him a ways," Race said
immediately.

Spade was in agreement with this. Scattering
the dying embers of the fire, they mounted and
set out after the herder. He was not losing any
time. They saw the white blur of his face when
he looked back at them. When he observed them
following, he changed his course and set out at a
lope.

"Well, let him go," Race said finally. "He's on
Fontana's range now."

They turned back, and had not gone more than
half-a-mile when a disturbance in a heavy patch
of willows along the north fork of the creek
attracted them.

"Something's in there," Race muttered. "Take
care it isn't another herder. . . . It's a horse!" he
added, when he had got a glimpse. "Saddled and
tethered!"

"Madriaga's!" Spade put in. "He was headin'
for here! He turned off when he seen us comin'
after him!"

Race was thoughtful. "So Madriaga lied," he
summed up. "You were right about him, Spade!"

"It don't do no good to say it now!" Spade

grumbled. "We had him—an' let him go."

Race was not troubled about that. "It's the best bait we've got, to let him feel safe," he pointed out. "Whether he's guilty or not, we haven't a thing on him right now. But we'll get it!" His tone was grim. "And when we do, it'll be just too bad for him—and for Fontana too!" he ended resolutely.

# Chapter XIX

## POKER FACE

Race Cullyer's pony pounded into the ranch yard from the Paradise road. He slid neatly out of the saddle near the open gate. The pony ran on down the yard, mane and tail flaunting.

Race entered the ranch house and found Fox in her favorite chair in the patio.

"We've got them!" he announced exultantly, waving a long envelope.

Fox's eyes sought first his face and then the envelope. "What have you, Race—the grazing permits?" She glowed with expectation, and the color in her cheeks made her beautiful.

He assented, slipping the permits from the envelope, he extended them, smiling at her eagerness as she unfolded them and scanned their contents.

"But Race!" she broke out in a startled tone. "Five thousand! We never can get that many sheep! Why, it would mean thirty or forty thousand dollars!"

He was sorry that he had deceived her as to his intentions. He hated sheep, and in his heart did not mean that they should run them. But he was in too deep to withdraw now.

"No," he admitted, "we couldn't swing that much money. If we run two thousand, we will be fortunate. All the same, those permits are our ace in the hole."

"But I fail to see—"

"You will see," he promised her. "Don't forget that the number of sheep that can be grazed on the Reserve is limited, the same as the number of cattle. Someone's fingers will be pinched this season. I'm expecting it to be Nick Fontana. It won't be long before he shows up to talk business. And unless I miss my guess, he'll be pretty wrathy!"

"And our own sheep?" Fox continued. "Do you intend to procure them through those extra permits?"

"That's the idea," he assented without a quiver.

There was an expression on Fox's face of fortitude, faith, and hope, despite her inevitable apprehensions.

"I have told you that I would believe in you," she said with feeling. "I wish that father could know. It is a plucky fight, and I am certain he would approve. I know of no other soul in the world who would stand by me as you are doing."

Race became suddenly grave.

"You know why I am doing it, don't you, Fox?" he asked quietly.

Her eyes were bright. "I do know. It is because you are what you are. You could do nothing else.

You think you are doing it for—" She broke off, reading the thought behind his intent face. "But what are we talking about?" she resumed, dissembling her confusion. She laughed practically, herself again in a moment.

Leaving the house a few minutes later, Race was rueful.

"What's got into me?" he growled. "Another minute of that and I would have had her in my arms! I better stop pushin' on the reins. She's got enough on her mind as it is."

True to Race's prediction, it was less than a week after the granting of the grazing permits before Nick Fontana put in an appearance. He was not as wrought up as Race had expected. Walking up to the ranch house with the sheepman, the foreman was reminded of the devious nature of the Basque.

Fontana chatted calmly about the fine appearance of the ranch. Race, however, had little to say. He was not deceived.

Fox led them to the office, as though to indicate that there was no mistake about this being a business meeting. Fontana rambled on after he had seated himself. It was obvious that he was sounding out their intentions.

"Naturally I'm interested in what you folks do," he said with apparent frankness. "Having a mortgage on the ranch, I like to know you're going in the right direction."

No one said anything for a moment, and Nick decided to make his hint more broad. "I hear in Paradise," he went on, "that you've decided to run sheep this year . . . but I guess that's a mistake, eh?"

"We have our permits to graze sheep on the Reserve," Fox told him calmly.

Nick's brows rose. "Yes?" he countered although he knew perfectly well that she had them. "So have I got mine," he went on levelly; "but you haven't made arrangements for your sheep yet?"

If he expected any explosion to follow his announcement that they had not beaten him out of grazing permits for his own sheep, he was disappointed.

"Why, yes," Race interposed before Fox had any opportunity to hesitate. "We've got our plans pushed pretty far along."

Nick read the bluff accurately. He did not miss the inference that it was none of his business how they stood in the matter.

"Well, that's fine," he said, his round olive face impassive. "But you're not counting your sheep before they've jumped the fence, have you? You can count on little or no help from the bank, you know."

"No," Race responded calmly, "we're not depending on the bank this time."

"It's a risky step for anyone who doesn't know

the business," Fontana continued pessimistically. "I don't want to see you disappointed." He was looking at Fox now. "Sheep are troublesome brutes. There's dipping them—shearers—herders to hire—a hundred and one things to be thought of. Of course if I can help you in any way. . . ." He waved a fat hand.

Watching him, Fox could not forget the advantage he had taken of her in the matter of the water from Soapstone Springs.

"We can manage all those things very well, Mr. Fontana," she told him.

"Well, you may meet with the unexpected," he persisted smoothly. He made a move to get up. "If you strike a hitch, or change your mind, come to me. I may be able to swing those permits— take them off your hands."

His whole manner was absent, but Race penetrated his object at once. It had been this speech—flung out, as it were, on the spur of the moment—for which the sheepman had come to the Diamond Bar. Fontana thought he could get their useless permits at his own price—as low as he wanted to make it.

"I reckon there won't be any necessity for that, Fontana," Race came back shortly. "And look here—" he pushed on, as Nick paused in the door, looking back; "I ran into one of your herders on our range the other afternoon. I warned him off—told him I didn't want to see him across the boundary again. I want you to hear that warning too."

For a moment the tension was electric. Then Fontana relaxed. He seemed even faintly aggrieved. "Well, of course I know how you feel, Cullyer. In spite of hot words, I've done everything I could to—"

"Just so long as you understand," Race cut him off evenly. "*I* don't want anything to come of this, either—but I don't want it left to me."

Fontana left without further speech.

"Now what?" she queried, watching his face. "I take it your plan went awry?"

"No," he temporized. "I did think I had Fontana out on a limb—but what about the other Basques? They'll feel the pinch. Don't worry, it will be all right."

He could not tell her his hope that the Basques, seeing themselves out-generaled, would get together and decide that their only course was to come forward. Much depended on the representative they sent to the Diamond Bar. The wrong man would ruin the one chance on which Race counted.

Fox took him at his word, and Race left it at that with an assumption of cheerful certainty. Nevertheless, it was a considerable relief to him when, the next afternoon, a second visitor arrived. It was old Angel Irosabel, of Paradise.

Irosabel was so old there was no telling his age.

181

He was a clean-cut, kindly-faced man, the best of his kind. His presence was a pleasing contrast to the treacherous atmosphere surrounding his compatriot, Nick Fontana, but he was a keen business man.

Fox took him to the patio, where the sun was warm and bright. Race accompanied them.

Straight-forward in his manner, old Angel came to the point of his visit at once.

"I wish to approach you about the sheep grazing permits you hold, Miss Hamlin," he began. "It was a clever move for you to increase the price of them. You won't run sheep yourself, of course. There can be no fiction about our need of them. I have come to ask your price."

Poker-faced, he was exhibiting the traditional policy of non-resistance of the Basques, who accepted defeat on every hand, and yet pushed ahead resistlessly, taking the blows passively and surmounting every one of them.

"You misunderstand, Mr. Irosabel," Fox told him quietly. "There has been no intention of taking advantage of your necessity. We are expecting to run sheep this year."

Old Angel's pretended surprise was deep. "Is that so?" he queried blankly. His eye strayed to Race as though by accident.

"Make no mistake, Mr. Irosabel," the latter put in, with a glance at Fox, who readily submitted. "Those permits are not for sale."

The old Basque collected himself. "But either you do not mean what you say, or you don't know what you are up against! What you have here is a cattle ranch. It would be practically impossible for you to make the switch—"

"Ordinarily, that would be true," Race took him up. "But we are in no position to weigh those considerations. . . . You know we have the permits to graze sheep on the Reserve. And you know too, that Fent Crocker has bought into the Lazy A, and snapped up the cattle-grazing permits that we would have depended on. We're in a pinch where there's no other way to turn. We've *got* to run sheep!"

"I see. But on the other hand, if you could get the cattle-grazing permits—?"

Race looked at him steadily, without speaking.

"You don't want to run sheep," Irosabel pointed out. "And at the same time we—my people, need the sheep grazing permits. Now if I were in a position to exchange your sheep permits for permits covering cattle . . . ?"

"Go on," Race invited.

"It happens," the sheepman explained deprecatorily, "that I own a controlling interest in the Lazy A."

Fox was taken aback, for this was news to her. It was not to Race, but he pretended a polite surprise.

"It might be," Irosabel went on smoothly, "that

I can persuade Crocker to release some of the permits he got with the idea of running cattle on shares. Would you—for this consideration—release the sheep grazing permits you hold?"

Race affected not to see Fox's suddenly raised hand.

"We might do that," he admitted levelly, "if we can agree all the way through."

Angel's grizzled brows rose. "I don't understand you."

Race extended a palm, and placed the forefinger of his other hand in the center of it. "We will trade you value for value in permits," he said carefully, "if you will extend us a loan with which to buy cattle sufficient to put the Diamond Bar back on its original basis."

Irosabel caressed his lips, his eyelids narrowed. "How many cattle would that mean?" he queried.

"Say a thousand head."

Old Angel stared at him without change of expression, but inwardly he was amazed at the other's cool effrontery. The extent of the foreman's gamble was colossal—and somehow admirable.

"This is handsome of you," the Basque responded with fine irony; "but you are asking for a loan of at least fifteen thousand dollars. I know nothing of the ranch's financial condition. . . ."

"The Diamond Bar is absolutely sound

collateral," Race pointed out firmly. "It has no more than a twenty-percent first mortgage on it, the interest of which has been kept up."

They talked it over for several moments before Irosabel finally shook his head.

"I couldn't do that," he decided.

"Very well." Race was calm. "We're right where we started. We'll run sheep."

Irosabel glanced at him with the caution of a cat ready to pounce on the mouse. "If you require a loan with which to buy cattle, what are you going to do for sheep?" he asked smoothly.

Race met his eye. "Maybe we can do business with Fontana," he responded.

Angel smiled grimly. "I have no doubt of it! To lend you more money is percisely what he most wishes to do . . . and you'll be playing right into his hands in the bargain!"

Race nodded, undismayed. "We'll do what we have to," he retorted. "There's every chance of our making enough money with the sheep to cut our obligation to him down."

Old Angel saw that he could make no impression on this square-jawed man. He took his departure with hardly suppressed irritation, but firm in his stand.

When he was gone, Fox turned quickly to Race.

"Race!" she exclaimed, at a loss. "Everything he says is true! . . . If Mr. Fontana should lend us money, he will be getting a death grip on the ranch!"

He nodded shortly. "That's agreed. But Fox, what are we to do? Cattle permits without cattle are of no use to anyone. At present, we hold something—these sheep permits—that others want badly. We've got to depend on them to bring us what we need. . . . Dealing with Fontana would be a desperate gamble; but when circumstances become desperate, you've got to get desperate with them!"

Fox's submission was not without its note of apprehension. "You are right too, of course. But I will be vastly relieved when I see a clear way out of this tangle, no matter what the cost!"

# Chapter XX

## RUMORS OF WAR

That evening, when Race stepped into the bunkhouse, he was well aware that the announcement he had to make might give rise to an explosion, but he did not let it deter him. It was winner take all, in the game he played.

Spade McSween greeted him. The buckaroos, gathered around the lamp-lit table on which a game of poker was in progress, let Spade's grunt do for them all.

Race watched the game for a moment. Baldy Crebo, sitting by himself on the edge of a bunk, hummed lowly on his jew's-harp for some time before he took it out of his mouth to inquire:

"You figurin' to get any more steers this spring, Race?"

"No." Race did not even bother to glance up. "We expect to run sheep for a season instead."

It elicited no comment for the minute, for Race's humor was dry. Not a one of them supposed he was in earnest.

Hank Leflett threw down his cards and leaned back. "I can picture myself herdin' sheep from the hurricane deck of a bronc," he commented,

187

pinching his tobacco sack as he poured out a smoke.

"You won't have to do it, Hank," Race told him quietly. "We're hirin' Basques—and the sheep will be up on the Reserve till some time in October."

Hank's chair came down with a bang.

"You don't mean this, Race!" he said levelly.

Stares of amazement were turned on the foreman.

"I do mean it," he assured them quietly.

Leflett's soft curse, in the midst of a profound quiet, sounded distinctly. "Sheep!" he ejaculated. "I'll be doubly damned!"

Race gazed back at him without expression. He was about to speak, when Spade cut him off:

"Lay off, Race! Enough is enough!" Race disillusioned him shortly.

"Sorry, boys. You can depend on your jobs as they are."

"Not by a damn sight!" Hank Leflett burst out. "I'll never depend on sheep fer no job of mine! I'll take my time first!"

"Wait a minute." Race held them all with his glance. "I'm not askin' you to do a thing you haven't been doin' right along. You won't have a thing to do with the sheep . . . I don't have to tell any of you how things stand. For the time bein' we're in a hole! Is that any reason for takin' it layin' down?"

"No!" Leflett retorted violently. "An' I can't see's it's any reason fer sellin' out to the boscos, either!"

The card game had broken up. The buckaroos stared at one another with expressions of amusement or disgust.

"We're not sellin' out, Hank," Race replied patiently.

"Yo're too willin' to wear a clothespin on yore nose to suit me," Leflett grumbled loudly. He was stamping back and forth by his bunk, collecting his belongings. A look of thunderous contempt overspread his features.

Having made ready his war-bag, Leflett confronted Race diffidently.

"I'll jest take my time now, Cullyer, if it's all the same to you," he declared.

Race nodded. "Come over to the house with me. I'll give you your check," he said quietly.

They started away, leaving a silence behind them which gave way to ejaculations as the buckaroos indulged in heated argument amongst themselves.

"I don't want anyone to think that we're goin' Basque because we've found it necessary to get a new foot-hold, Leflett," Race remarked as he made out the other's check at his desk in the cottage.

"Reckon a lot of fellers've said that in this country in the past," Hank countered without

189

interest. "They're all livin' somewhere's else now."

Race saw that he could get nowhere with the man. He handed over the check in silence. Leflett accepted it and left without a word.

Race did not make the mistake of returning to the bunkhouse. The buckaroos must be given their chance to argue the matter out by themselves. He had his own reasons for making them think they must reconcile themselves to the prospect of sheep on the ranch.

Great as his faith in his partner was, Spade McSween had little to say to Race the following morning. He glanced at him with puzzlement in his eyes, and showed no interest in the other's movements. Thus it was that the foreman was alone when, during the course of the morning, he rode out to visit the overflow ditch from Soapstone Springs.

He was delighted to find a trickle of water coursing the rocky bed of the stream. Small as it was, he knew that it would grow in time to its old proportions.

He lost no time in riding back to the ranch and acquainting Fox Hamlin with his discovery.

"That's excellent news, Race!" she responded, her eyes brightening. "We'll have water on the upper alfalfa field this year, after all."

"Yes, but it'll be too late to do any good for a first crop, I'm afraid," he told her. "The best we can hope for is half a crop in the early fall."

"But that's a great deal better than nothing at all from that ground! . . . And it will give us the stubble to use early next winter," she discovered. "Are you reasonably sure the water will continue to come, Race? Mr. Fontana will not do anything about his useless pipe line?"

"I don't know what he can do," he reassured her. "He will be quick enough to gather what has happened, but where does that leave him? The pipe was buried to save it from freezing. And if he dug it up, there would always be the chance of the same process repeating itself. . . . No," he concluded; "Fontana will charge his expensive pipe line up to profit and loss, and end by letting us have the water from the spring!"

That afternoon Race returned to his work. The buckaroos had learned about the trickle of water from the springs. That they might think him absorbed in that development, he rode again in that direction. Returning to the ranch he was in time to walk in on a group of cattlemen who had called on Fox.

They were in the patio, and only Fox and old Sam Taylor, a close friend of Luke Hamlin before the latter's demise, were seated. The others were on their feet, hands behind their backs and a discontented scowl on most of their faces.

A brief silence fell at the entrance of the foreman, broken only by the brusque greetings tendered him. The first speech thereafter was enough to acquaint him with what was afoot.

"I tell you, the sheep is jest asweepin' over this country!" Rankin, of the Frying Pan, resumed, obviously where he had left off. "But it ain't that alone that bothers us—even the money is goin' there too! You say you can't make the riffle as things are—but ma'am, it ain't goin' to help none to put what money you do git aholt of into sheep!"

"Rankin, I'll answer that for you," Race interposed. "Could Miss Hamlin get any financial help from any of you hard-shell ranchers right now? No! Could she get any from cattlemen's bank either? You know the answer to that too! It's a sheepman that she expects to get her money from, and in view of that, you men haven't a right to peep!"

The ranchers muttered at this, their disapproval plain. Rankin went so far as to bluster:

"That's all right, Cullyer; but Miss Hamlin don't understand this like a cowman would! Her father was talkin' to me the very mornin' he died—an' it was agin' exactly this! I tell you, yo're deliverin' another cattle spread over to the boscos! More acres for bronco grass!"

"Yes—an' don't fergit, yo're startin' somethin'

that's been started before in this country, an allus come to the same end!" Steve Slegel, another rancher thrust in.

Race waited until the cattlemen had shot their bolts, meeting them with brief responses calculated to bring them up short. They took his meaning fully. It was not long before they began to drift toward the ranch yard.

Fox saw them off with quiet decision but there was no mistaking the preoccupation in her regard when she turned to Race.

"Those men certainly put up a determined protest," she remarked. "Leflett is spreading the story broadcast that we will run sheep."

"Well, there's nothing to worry about, Fox. . . . Don't let these old die-hards affect you. They mean well, but they can see nothing except their own way. . . . I shall have to go and see Fontana shortly. We will soon be standing on our own feet again."

"I know—and I am glad. But these presages of trouble worry me. . . . Race, are you thoroughly convinced of the soundness of what you propose?"

He was glad she had put it that way. "Absolutely," he answered.

Fox sighed. "Then I will be content. . . . There remains only the proof of time to carry your point. Race, I hope—I pray you may be right!"

He accepted her acquiescence like an

accusation. It would have been impossible now to tell her it was upon these presages of trouble that the efficacy of his stratagem rested. No other course would so quickly convince Angel Irosabel of his decision to run sheep.

# Chapter XXI

## POWDER SMOKE

Four ponies wearing the Diamond Bar brand carried their riders within the shade of the poplars, and at the corner, the main street of Paradise opened up before them. It appeared unwontedly deserted, as had the yards of the houses where ordinarily many Basque children played. There was no ignoring the growing air of tension that held the little village.

"Somethin's wrong here," Stub Varian volunteered in an undertone. "What in hell is it?"

"Wal, you couldn't expect these folks to be tickled over a cattle ranch takin' to sheep," Pop Devore muttered. "This here's how they're takin' it!"

Race glanced at him briefly without speaking. It would have been greatly to his benefit if this were the case, but he was cautious of leaping to the desirable supposition.

It was Spade McSween who accosted a storekeeper as they swung out of the saddles before Benavides's saloon. The merchant paused in his door, and Spade stepped forward, to talk to him in low tones. Then Spade nodded his head, laughed shortly, and turned to join his fellows.

"It's Blaney," he explained. "He's in town lickered up, madder'n a wet wolf, an' makin' his brag that he's out to git Fontana."

"Fontana!" Stub ejaculated guardedly, glancing about. "That's damn queer!"

Spade's eyes gleamed. "It ain't so queer," he denied. "Blaney claims the bosco double-crossed him on his grazin' permits. He got left out in the cold. He's out fer blood!"

Pop Devore's fleeting glance to Race's face was quizzical. "Blast you, Race!" he put in half-admiringly. "You got *yore* permits to run sheep up there! Was you figurin' on some such outcome as this?"

"Somebody had to get left behind," Race responded laconically.

They turned into the saloon. It was empty except for the bartender and Hank Leflett. Hank hung over the far end of the bar, a cigarette in his fingers.

"Hey, Hank!" Stub Varian greeted him as though nothing had happened. "C'mon over here an' have a drink with us."

Varian and his companions had bellied up to the bar. Leflett glanced at them sidelong, half-amused and half-resentful.

"I don't know whether I want to drink with a bunch of sheep-herders or not," he responded.

The Diamond Bar buckaroos were unruffled.

"You come to the wrong bar, then, if that's the

case," Pop Devore retorted tolerantly. He did not glance up at the Basque bartender, who slid out the glasses in silence and stared at them out of flinty black eyes.

Leflett continued to twit them about the sheep. Varian and Devore answered him with stoic calm. Race and Spade were engaged in low-voiced conversation over their glasses.

"Damn you, Race!" Spade muttered his exasperation. "You ain't goin' through with this! Here you go gettin' these boys all riled up, an' it don't mean a blame thing! . . . When're you goin' to crack?"

It was a question that Race had been asking himself. Angel Irosabel had shown no sign of weakening, remaining severely to himself. It gave rise to an inner tension greater than that which gripped Paradise at the present moment, but Race was far from divulging it.

"I'll never crack," he said shortly.

Spade growled in his throat, as much disgusted with Race's duplicity as he would have been to learn that the Diamond Bar was indeed to run sheep.

No one had heard their exchange. Race glanced up as a heavy man entered and passed behind them on his way to the bar. He saw that it was Blaney. Others looked also, and a heavy silence fell in the saloon in which Blaney's steps sounded loudly.

The sheepman's deep-lined face was savage. He had been drinking heavily. This added fuel to his initial resentment, and his burning eyes and flushed features reflected a cauldron of rage and hatred. There could be no doubt from his manner that he meant to wreak violence on the person of Nick Fontana.

He ignored the buckaroos, heading for the unoccupied portion of the bar and demanding whisky in a tone that made the Basque start. So unconsciously theatrical was it that it broke the tension.

"No, I ain't even decided if I *want* 'nother job in this damn country," Leflett resumed his banter.

"That's shore a thought," Stub Varian countered, apparently addressing the ceiling. "It does pay to find out if yo're considered a desir'ble citizen before you settle anywheres."

"Then on the other hand," Hank flung back, "if yo're a sheep-herder you don't have to worry. Yo're so God-forsaken, nobody pays any 'ttention to you."

If Blaney heard any of this he gave no sign, staring into his glass with moody fierceness, and stealing glances toward the door.

" 'For I'm only a pore cowboy,' " Stub raised his voice complacently in song, " 'an' I know I done wrong!' "

That it served very well as a rejoinder was evident. Leflett's answer was sharp.

"There is a satisfaction in doin' what you damn please, even if you know it's wrong," he told the bartender. "I'd rather shoot a dozen sheepherders than desert one cow!"

The Basque stared back blankly, his silent antagonism plain. It was Blaney who reared up sharply, his malevolent eye swiveling on Leflett.

"Here's one you can shoot, you damned cow-prod—if you're good enough!" he snarled vindictively. His hands flashed before Hank had made a move, and two shining .45s appeared in his grasp.

"Hold on, there!" Race thrust in, snapping his words at Blaney's broad back. "Don't get gay, Blaney, because you're on the peck!"

Crouched and ready, Blaney sidled to the center of the room, where he had a partial view of the entire bar. He kept on until he had all five of the punchers roughly in a row before him.

"I'm ready to take you on too, Cullyer—an' all yore friends!" the big sheepman blazed. "You think you can come in here an' run this town to suit yoreself! That's where yo're wrong!"

The four Diamond Bar men faced him with deceptive indolence, backs to the bar, their hands idle. Even Hank Leflett had turned, his arm hanging in readiness.

"You ain't so much—the whole pack of you!" Blaney went on in a cold fury, his guns unwavering. "You think yo're tough, but you wasn't so much when Win Flood got knocked off—or old man Hamlin either! Why don't you do somethin' about the man that got them?"

Race knew that the sheepman's consuming rage against Fontana swayed him. He grasped at the implied accusation eagerly. Did Blaney know anything?

No one said anything after Blaney's furious outburst. All knew the killer's mood that was on him. It would be foolish to provoke it deliberately.

Blaney gave them a final contemptuous glare and slid crabwise through the door.

A grunt from Spade McSween was the only expression that marked his departure. It was cut off by Pop Devore's exclamation as he peered through the window.

"Now we'll see somethin' doin'! Look there!" His tone was portentous.

Race saw the figures of two men across the street who spelled imminent trouble. They were Nick Fontana and Ramon Madriaga.

Simultaneously with this discovery came the hoarse sound of Blaney's call. The buckaroos crowded to the door to watch. Hank Leflett was intrigued into joining them, forgetting his split with the outfit in the tension of the moment.

"Damn you, Fontana—I been lookin' fer you!" Blaney roared, stalking forward, his huge shoulders swaying.

The stout Basque faced him without visible emotion. He and Madriaga came forward calmly. The three men met in the middle of the street and stopped.

"What do you want of me, Blaney?" Nick queried directly, his black eyes unwavering.

"You know what I want!" the raw-boned American flared. "You double-crossed me on my grazin' permits, blast yore soul! Now what're you goin' to do about it?"

"What are you driving at?" Fontana countered with irritation. "I take care of my own business, Blaney. Can I help yours going wrong?"

"You got permits fer more sheep'n you ever run on the Reserve before!" Blaney bellowed. "Did you let anybody else know what you was doin'? No! An' you'll answer to me fer it!"

Fontana turned cold and wary. He did not remove his gaze from Blaney's bloated face.

"I told you—" he began gratingly.

"You ain't tell' me anything!" Blaney cut him off furiously. "I'm tellin' you, Bosco! I played yore game too long to be throwed down now! . . . Are you goin' to hand over my share of them permits?"

Fontana stared at him, noncommittal.

"Think it over damn serious!" Blaney directed bitterly. "Balk me, Fontana, an' it'll go hard with you! I got ways of dealin' with you!"

"Name one!" the Basque snapped flatly.

201

"Here's one, right here!" Blaney flamed at him, tapping the stock of one of his six-guns. "An' there's a little matter of yore own guns that might come in handy!"

"Come to cases!" Fontana told him sharply.

"I c'n do that too! . . . How 'bout Win Flood, Fontana? You sneaked that once; but I know what I know! An' how 'bout Luke Hamlin, while I'm about it?"

Nick's eyes narrowed. "I don't know anything about it," he retorted doggedly. "Don't try to scare me, Blaney! What has this to do with grazing permits?"

"Nemmine what!" Blaney caught him up heatedly, whipping himself to the point of action. "You know what, all right!" He swung toward Madriaga. "I don't s'pose Madriaga knows about them two fellers either!" he charged scathingly. "I'll turn up the two of you!"

Madriaga showed signs of nervousness, Fontana put a hand on his arm. "Go away, Ramon," he ordered gutturally. "I'll take care of this!"

After one venomous stare at Blaney, Madriaga turned to leave.

"Wait a minute, there!" Hank Leflett barked. "I want to talk to you, young feller!" He had known Win Flood well, and did not propose to forget him now. He started toward Madriaga, his six-gun coming out.

Fontana saw it in a flash. His own hand moved. Watching the Basque like a hawk, Blaney went into action.

Three shots rang out in rapid succession, to be followed an instant later by a fourth.

Blaney's useless slug ploughed up the dirt at Fontana's feet. The big American jerked and buckled, to come down like a chopped tree, dead when he hit the ground.

The third shot—Hank Leflett's, at the disappearing figure of Ramon Madriaga—had missed; but the delayed fourth, Fontana's, cut down the buckaroo in his stride. Hank sprawled awkwardly and lay still.

The Diamond Bar men rushed forward with hoarse cries. Race was at the fore as they faced Fontana. For a moment anything could happen.

Then Fontana straightened, putting up his gun, his face flinty.

"I'm glad you saw this, Cullyer!" he said gruffly. "You'll be able to testify that I did it in self-defense!"

Race's gaze was keen. "I can do that—in Blaney's case. But I'm not so sure that Luke Hamlin was killed in self-defense!"

Nick's bushy brows twitched. "What do you mean by that?"

"You get me!" Race retorted. "I seem to have stumbled onto a way to smoke you out, with this grazing permit tangle. It's too bad Blaney won't ever be able to testify. But we're getting somewhere now!"

"You're welcome to wherever it will get you," Fontana said shortly, turning away.

"Wait a minute, Fontana!" Race brought him back. A fleeting glance at the crowd that had collected showed him old Angel Irosabel, taking in the belligerent exchanges with a satisfied expression. It gave Race an idea.

"I'm not foolin' myself about you," he told Nick grimly. "This sheep business is provin' fatal to man after man, and these two bring up the total to five! I'm for makin' an end of it here and now. Maybe we can make a deal!"

The murmuring in the crowd stilled. Even the buckaroos were staring at Race as though petrified. Fontana stood pat, watching him steadily.

"Name your deal," he invited shortly.

"I'll do that. I've got sheep permits—and I want to get rid of 'em in a hurry—wash my hands of the business." Race's face was hard, for he was conscious of the disgusted stares directed at him. But he had no intention of shirking the bold stroke he meant to play. "Are you still willing to buy?"

"It depends on what you're asking," Fontana rejoined.

"We'll talk that over. I can't say what my price would be, beyond a small profit."

Fontana paid no more attention than Race to the contempt of the auditors for this haggling.

"Maybe it'll be at my price," he suggested.

"That remains to be seen," Race closed the discussion. "I'll be over to your place tomorrow noon. We can thrash it out."

He did not catch Fontana's nod, striving to catch Angel Irosabel's reaction to the affair. The old Basque was disturbed. He shook his head, moving away.

The buckaroos had gathered around Hank Leflett and were examining him.

"He ain't dead!" Pop Devore averred. "Fontana's slug got him in the shoulder—a clean bore."

Someone brought whisky. It was poured down Hank's throat, and in another moment he opened his eyes.

"Where am I?" he gasped weakly.

Stub Varian laughed gruffly. "Yo're on yore way back to the Diamond Bar to get well!" he answered. "Go hunt up a wagon to move him in, somebody!"

He glanced at Race for confirmation as he spoke, and the latter nodded. Spade McSween stumped away toward the livery barn.

"No sir, by God!" Leflett angrily argued. "I ain't agoin' back to that place—you hear me!"

"Blast you, lay still!" Varian told him bluntly.

"D'you want to bleed to death? . . . Yo're goin' back there, an' yo're goin' to like it! You might's well get used to the idea!"

Leflett groaned helplessly and subsided.

# Chapter XXII

## CAUTIOUS AS A WOLF

Hank Leflett was taken back to the Diamond Bar and made comfortable in the bunkhouse. He was even more querulous than the usual sufferer from gun-shot wound, and bade fair to wear out the patience of all before an hour had passed. He knew what he was doing. To his way of it, the boys had toted him off while he lay helpless and suffering, and he meant to make them pay for it in the only way he knew how.

"Take it easy, Hank!" Baldy Crebo wailed at him after a solid ten minutes of complaint. "You gotta be looked after, ain't you? D'you think anybody in Paradise would'a looked out fer you? You'd be layin' in a livery stall now, smellin' harness and hay, if it wasn't fer us!"

"Wal, I c'n blow off a little if I wanta! I'd rather *be* in a stable! Dang it all, I c'n smell sheep here already!"

"Yo're a liar!" Pop Devore snapped back at him. "What you smell is that fool move you made in town, an' you know it! I c'n smell it myself! You don't have to go blamin' it on sheep!"

It was the first time anyone had taken refuge in anything but patient argument with Leflett,

207

and it silenced him effectually for five minutes. Thereafter, having been shown the way, the cowboys blasted him with ridicule every time he effected to whine. Scenting the drift of affairs, Hank came back at them with interest, his indignation aroused. The bunkhouse rocked with outrageous personalities.

"This is a fine way to be takin' care of a feller!" Hank blustered scathingly at last. "What you doin'—keepin' my tail up fer me? I never saw such a damn bunch of punks!"

For once, it elicited no acid rejoinder, and Hank's eyes drifted around surprisedly. The buckaroos sat in uncomfortable silence, gazing at the door. In it stood Fox Hamlin, her face slightly flushed, her glance quizzical.

"I'm afraid you are taking too good care of the—patient," she told them. "Is it necessary to raise his temperature?"

"No-o, ma'am!"—"We wouldn't do that!"—"He's comin' out of it gradual, ma'am!" the embarrassed rejoinders sounded.

Fox came forward to see whether she could do anything for Leflett's comfort. One after another of the punchers departed with a crestfallen air, as though they had been caught in deviltry.

"Shucks, ma'am, we was jest chewin'!" Hank mumbled.

"I know. But you must have quiet. Are you comfortable?" she inquired.

Hank was flustered, ashamed now for the things he had said about sheep in the past ten minutes. Had she heard any of them? Her face, curiously composed as though by an effort, seemed to indicate that she had. Leflett fell silent, and Fox got little more out of him for the duration of her visit.

Race Cullyer scarcely went near Hank after he was installed in his old bunk. The foreman had been conscious of a tightening manner toward him since his deliberate dickering with Fontana in Paradise, across the dead body of Blaney. He knew the men disapproved of his dealing with the Basque, despite his declaration that he wanted to be rid of the sheep permits and everything connected with them.

Spade McSween showed his loyalty here, breaking the silence in which the others had left Race.

"Blame it all, Race!" he growled that evening; "now you've scrambled this thing fer fair! I *knowed* you wouldn't have anythin' to do with sheep—but why crack when you did? The boys got the notion yo're givin' up. That's worse than bein' bull-headed!"

"It wasn't the boys I wanted to think I was giving up," Race answered him levelly. "You sit tight, Spade, and watch the game. Somebody's due to call this hand in short order!"

Spade swore under his breath. "Damn yore

eyes!" he exploded admiringly. "I knowed all the while you had a game somewheres!"

But Race was restless as the night wore on. There were too many chances that his expectations would fail to materialize, and as he conned them, it seemed that morning would never come. When it did, it was disappointingly calm. The foreman gave no sign of his own tension when, at ten o'clock, he answered a call from Fox and went up to the house.

"What are you going to do, Race?" she greeted him seriously. "Are you going to see Mr. Fontana today?" She had heard about the shooting-scrape in Paradise, Race had not held back from her the proposal he had made to the stout Basque.

"We will have to do something before long," he told her plainly.

They talked it over soberly at some length. Race was beginning to feel that his bluff had been called, when old Inez shuffled in to announce the arrival of a visitor. Getting up, Fox followed her out.

A moment later, Angel Irosabel stepped into the patio. The old Basque accepted a seat.

"I have come back, señor, to ask whether your offer is still open?" he inquired of Race. Polite as he was to Fox, there was no doubt in his mind whom he must do business with here.

"I take it you still desire the sheep grazing

permits?" Race countered. He scarcely dared glance at Fox.

Irosabel assented. "I would rather have them at the cost of a loan, from you, than get them from—another gentleman whose price would be exorbitant."

"Then it can be arranged," Race countered, "on the terms we discussed previously."

"And those were—?"

"Exchange of sheep permits for permits covering two thousand head of cattle," Race stipulated; "an adjustment of grazing-fee differences, and a loan which will permit us to buy a thousand head of steers—say fifteen thousand dollars." He said nothing of the blow this exchange of grazing permits would be to Fent Crocker, but he was savoring its justice.

Angel Irosabel lowered his head as though taking a particularly bitter draught. Then he looked up. "I agree to those terms," he said simply.

Fox's amazement at this unexpected good fortune was keen.

"Mr. Irosabel—this is kind of you!" she said frankly.

Old Angel glanced at her. "Perhaps. I am not doing it for kindness' sake, however," he replied dryly.

Fox's eye strayed to Race with sudden understanding. Had *he* known this was finally to come about? Had he planned it? Her growing conviction that such was the case held her taut with wonderment. She felt the gush of a comforting warmth toward him. Then she concentrated her attention as the men went on to discuss the terms of the loan.

"If you will pardon me," Irosabel explained suavely, "I have sent one of my young men in to Winnemucca for my attorney. He should be here in an hour or two. If it is agreeable to you, we will complete the transaction at once."

"Certainly," Race agreed as gravely.

Once the details of business were settled, old Angel relaxed, talking about their chances of success. The time passed almost with celerity, yet it was a relief to Fox and Race when Irosabel's attorney arrived and was shown in.

The papers were drawn up and signed. Irosabel's check was put away in the ranch safe; and only then was Fox conscious of a let-up of suspense. Not since she had become the owner of the Diamond Bar had she experienced the confidence which she enjoyed now.

It was mid-afternoon by the time the transaction was completed. Irosabel and his lawyer made ready to take their departure. Race accompanied them to the ranch yard.

They were about to leave when a lathered pony stamped up the ranch road and drew in at the gate. Its rider was Nick Fontana, his ordinarily serene face clamped down in lines of anger when his eye lighted upon Angel Irosabel. He bored Race with a severe glare.

"I thought you were coming to see me at noon!" he charged.

"I changed my mind, Fontana," Race told him.

"Damn you, Irosabel!" Nick went on, coldly furious. "You heard that appointment made! You deliberately came here to cut my throat!" He burst into a gushing tirade of Spanish, which broke against the iron in old Angel's passive nature like an ineffectual tide against rocks.

"That's enough, Fontana!" Race broke in sharply. "We know why Irosabel beat you to the throw! He did it so you couldn't cut *his* throat on those permits! . . . Now you get me, and get me right! I've stood enough from you, in one way or another! You get back over my range line in a hurry, and don't you come across it again while I'm foreman of this ranch!"

His plangent voice carried to the door of the ranch house where Fox stood listening with blanched face. The buckaroos were observing the affair from the corrals, their grins masked.

Fontana snarled in his throat, his features darkening to plum color. But there was nothing that he could say. He glared at Race and then at Irosabel. With an exasperated curse yanked his pony's head around and rode away, the gravel flying.

"Thank you, señor," said old Angel unemotionally.

In another minute he and his attorney had departed. Race walked back to join Fox.

"This is the result I have been angling for," he said, as they walked back to the patio to discuss their altered situation. "The ranch is okay now. We will have our cattle, and we'll be able to put them on the Reserve in the bargain. . . . I'll have to apologize for keeping you in the dark for a while, Fox. I saw no other way to do it. We *might* have had to run sheep!"

She laughed lowly. "I don't think I would have been afraid of the outcome—even of that, with you in charge of the ranch," she assured him loyally.

That evening, Spade McSween sought out Race and accosted him frankly.

"Race, I never seen a smoother game worked in my life," he said admiringly. "If I ever run acrost a man, wants to squeeze somethin' out of nothin', I'll send him to you."

"Don't fool yourself," Race replied seriously. "It looks like we're in clover now, but there's one or two people we've got to deal with yet."

"Shore!" Spade countered gruffly; "but you've reckoned with 'em in the past. I'm layin' my bets on you, feller!"

"That may be, but a man can slip up once in a while," Race persisted, his face sober. "Spade,

Crocker's going to be so peeved about this he could chew nails! Fontana didn't come over here just to cuss and blow, either. . . . I tell you there's going to be a kick-back from this!"

"Well, if you're figurin' that way, you're a jump or two ahead of folks yet," Spade assured, undisturbed. "Man, you're as cautious as a wolf! I'll jest string along with you. It ought to be right interestin' to watch!"

# Chapter XXIII

## "COME CLEAN!"

Spade's acceptance of Race Cullyer's warning was intensely practical, like everything else about the club-footed puncher. He visioned the animosity of Fent Crocker and Nick Fontana as an active and virulent force; and although he said nothing about it, he pitted himself against it with deliberate intent.

If anyone noticed that Spade stayed to himself, it was not mentioned. He did not advertise the extra riding he did, for it was done swiftly, and along portions of the range line where he was not likely to be seen.

Nevertheless, it was almost pure accident that tumbled him into adventure the next evening. It was gathering dusk, and he was riding in from his lonely vigil along the boundary, his pony plodding along quietly, when he beheld a darting shadow within a hundred yards of the ranch house. He was instantly alert.

It could not have been a coyote. No desert dog would have been prowling in the shadow of the unused root cellar—a heaped-up earthen mound, with a sunken door.

Jabbing the spurs home, Spade sent his pony

lunging toward the sage clump into which the shade had faded. A sharp rustle preceded him, and an unguarded gasp, above the pound of the pony's hoofs and the squeal of saddle-leather. Then in an open space ahead, the puncher saw a running form.

The cow pony thrashed after through the sage. As Spade made a long grab, the fugitive dodged sidewise. Growling a curse, Spade kicked loose from the stirrups. When the pony sprang close once more, he left the saddle in a flying leap, to come down on his panting quarry with a crash.

It was over in a second. The other was smaller and lighter than Spade. The rifle which he had attempted desperately to swing around in his stride, was knocked yards away into the sage by Spade's savage swing. Together the two groveled on the ground.

When his captive became still, Spade clambered up and yanked him to his feet, peering into his face. It was Ramon Madriaga. Suddenly enraged by the discovery, Spade shook him until his teeth rattled.

"What in blazes 're you doin' here?" he bit out.

The Basque was sullenly silent. Spade needed no answer to inform him that Madriaga had come with violence in his heart toward Race Cullyer.

"Speak up!" Spade ordered gruffly, giving him a slap.

Ramon only panted, staring from under lowered brows, his black eyes glaring defiance.

"So you won't talk, eh?" Spade rumbled. "By God, you'll talk for me, or you'll never speak again!"

He began to yank Madriaga toward the root cellar, his grim plan taking shape in his mind. The young Basque was plainly terrified, struggling fruitlessly; but he maintained his silence.

They reached the root cellar and stumbled through the doorway. Spade flung his prisoner into a corner and struck a match. With Madriaga watching like a cornered beast, the puncher lit a smoky lantern hanging from a stake driven into the dirt wall. Its illumination was weak at best, but it was enough to show the harsh set of Spade's face. Madriaga cowered away from him in his corner.

"Now, will you come acrost, or will I make you?" Spade grated. He jerked Madriaga up and confronted him menacingly. "What was you here for? Was it to get Race?"

Ramon only glared. Spade flung blows at him with aroused fury. "You're givin' yoreself an awful beatin' before you talk!" he warned. And after a few more cuffs: "What d'you know about Luke Hamlin dyin', eh?"

Fear dawned in Madriaga's eyes. It grew as his punishment went on. Still he maintained a stubborn silence. Spade beat him until he was tired, and got nothing out of him. Exasperated, the puncher felled him with a single blow which bloodied his face. Then he pulled him upright once more.

"Now, talk!" he gritted, his fist poised again.

"No," Madriaga moaned.

Spade gave it up. "All right! You'll stay where you are—an' you don't eat till you do talk!"

Unceremoniously he bound and gagged the herder securely, paying no attention to the other's groans. Dropping his captive on some sacking, Spade blew out the lantern, and stepping out, closed the door.

"He'll talk!" he promised himself, slapping the dust from his clothes as he went after Madriaga's rifle and his own pony. Evidently the Basque had had no horse, unless he had left it tethered somewhere while he sneaked up on foot. "I'll have a look tomorrow," Spade decided. "Lucky for me it was dark when I nailed him, plumb in sight of the house like that! If Race knowed I had the skunk, he'd say to let him go. I'll let him go—like hell!"

True to his intention, Spade said nothing to anyone of his captive. On the following morning he searched diligently for any pony the herder might have left concealed, but found none. Thereafter, he kept a watch in the direction of Fontana's range, waiting for anyone who might trail Madriaga.

He stayed away from the unused cellar except at such times as it was unlikely that others could know where he was. When he did return, it was to find Madriaga as obdurate as ever.

"Does Fontana know you come over here to plug Race?" he demanded. "Is he likely to be wonderin' where you are? . . . Why don't you squawk, you knot-head? You ain't savin' yoreself nothin' by buttonin' that mean lip of yours!"

Ramon only glowered at him with growing listlessness as the hours lengthened, but with undiminished defiance.

"Yo're jest pilin' up grief for yoreself!" Spade goaded him mercilessly. "It's plumb up to you how hungry you get before you crack. You'll either crack or croak!"

Fire leapt into Madriaga's stare at the brutal levity, but he said nothing, submitting to the gag again before Spade left him, with stoic belligerence.

Spade veiled his vigilance and his nightly attacks on Madriaga's armor of silence with a manner of casualness when he was amongst the buckaroos. It was successful to a degree, and would have continued so, had he not overlooked one thing, minute in itself, but with definite consequences.

It was during the evening of the second day of Madriaga's imprisonment that Race became aware of an atmosphere of mystery on the ranch which he could not fathom. He studied it with his usual calm detachment, but was unable to detect any positive signs that something was wrong.

Stepping into the bunkhouse that night, he attuned his attention to small details, masking it under a preoccupied manner.

Spade caught it, however. It made him doubly cautious. "He smells a rat," he told himself, his instincts suddenly alive. "I got to put him off!"

Accordingly, he complained gruffly of the convalescent vagaries of Hank Leflett, until Race turned away as though to escape him.

Outside, however, the foreman paused as a new thought struck him. "Spade!" he murmured to himself. "He's the one that's been different. This is the first time he's belly-ached to me for two-three days—the first he's been around to do it!"

He went back to his cottage thoughtfully, determined to check up on the puncher. It was the next evening before the work gave him sufficient leisure to put his plan into effect.

Leaving the dining-room immediately after supper, having mentioned casually in the hearing of the buckaroos that he meant to do some figuring, Race waited until the lamp flashed on the bunkhouse, although it was not yet dark. Then he stepped over.

"Where's Spade?" he queried offhandedly from the door, after first ascertaining that the other was not present.

221

"Don't know," said Slim Browder.

"He's out monkeyin' in the harness shed," Baldy Crebo volunteered. "Patchin' a bridle rein or somethin', Race."

Race bent his steps toward the shed, an isolated one near the milking corral. The wind was rising, the sky overcast. He watched the signs in the dust as he went. Spade's clubbed foot left a trail easily read. The marks passed the harness shed and turned off in another direction.

"He *has* got something up his sleeve!" Race mused, his interest quickening.

Meanwhile, Spade had left the supper table, grumbling about his bridle, and made his way by a devious route to the unused cellar. Ordinarily he would have waited; but something told him that he had not much time now.

Madriaga looked haggard, his eyes sunken and lustreless, when Spade lit the lantern.

"Well!" Spade greeted him sternly, removing the gag, "are you goin' to talk, or are you goin' to starve along fer another day?"

Ramon opened his mouth, then shut it without speech. He was a different man from the insolent herder Spade had nabbed three nights ago. It was not hunger that drove him to submission, however, but raging thirst. Already his tongue had begun to swell.

"What you—want to know?" he muttered at last, with difficulty.

"Ready to speak up now, eh?" Spade masked his exultation. "Here's one you can answer—did Fontana send you here after Race?"

"No."

"Oh, no? Mebbe you forgot the answer. . . . But you was after him, just the same, wasn't you?"

Ramon's sullen silence was a sufficient affirmative.

"You knocked off Win Flood too, didn't you?" Spade bored on.

Madriaga wavered. "He killed my father," he muttered finally.

"What was the reason you plugged Luke Hamlin?" Spade suddenly shot at him. "You did—didn't you?"

Ramon's eyes showed terror.

"Come clean!" Spade rasped, raising a threatening fist.

"Ye-yes!" the Basque chattered.

Spade nodded hardily. "So you had a reason for that—an' for shootin' our steers too, eh? . . . How much did Fontana pay you for them jobs?"

Ramon turned white and shut his eyes. He had suddenly decided to shut up. Spade swore at him and threatened him to no purpose. He was about to replace the gag in Madriaga's mouth when the Basque shook a vigorous negative.

"No—wait—I talk!" he promised.

"Spit it out, then! Fontana *did* pay you for pluggin' Hamlin, didn't he?"

Ramon could not say it. His head jerked assent.

Spade was grimly pleased with himself. "Well, we got that far, then! Now how about—"

At this moment a step sounded in the door. A gust entered as it was swung back. Spade's hand jerked at the same time, and when Race came into the light of the lantern it was to meet the menacing muzzle of a six-gun.

"What have you got here, Spade? How long has this been goin' on?" he demanded, staring in surprise at Madriaga's trussed-up form.

Spade lowered the .45 and turned to look down at Ramon also, his manner grim.

"Ain't he a pretty sight?" he queried shortly.

Madriaga was. His clothes were disheveled from his useless struggles; his face was thin and hollow, and smeared with blood; his eyes were sunk in his head. He looked the picture of dejection and defeat.

"Race, I knowed you wouldn't let me do this if you caught on," Spade explained frankly. "This rat jest come through for me—confessed to drilling Luke Hamlin—everything!"

The foreman's surprise doubled. Spade told him the story of Madriaga's capture, and detailed the young Basque's admissions.

"Wait up with that!" Race broke in then. "We'll just get it on paper!"

He drew out a tally-book and pencil, and took down the bald narrative of crime and vengeance which Madriaga was now willing to divulge.

"Untie his arms and hands," Race directed, when it was done. "Now sign this, Madriaga!" he snapped.

Ramon did so.

"Take off some of that rope, and let him have some comfort," Race went on, straightening. "Get him some water, and give him food too. He's weak; he can't do much. Tomorrow we'll take him in to the sheriff."

Spade nodded. A moment later the two men were moving back toward the ranch through the blustery darkness.

"Fontana and Madriaga will both get it for this," Race declared. "I can't approve of your methods, Spade; but I've sure got to thank you for the results."

Spade left him to see to Madriaga's care. Race lost no time in seeking Fox Hamlin at the house. He found her in the office.

She met him with a smile, which faded as his story of Madriaga's capture and confessions unfolded.

"This must be taken care of at once," she said decidedly. "Why, that herder must have intended an attempt on your life, Race, when he was caught!"

They talked the affair over at length. Finally Race attempted to steer away from the subject, Fox followed willingly, but she had been reminded so strongly of her father again that she could not put him out of her thoughts.

"We'll have to be getting our new stock soon," Race began. "I've been thinking about getting them over in the Owyhee country. Some of those big ranches along the river should have what we want."

"Father bought cattle over there once or twice," Fox remembered, her face wistful. "Poor daddy! . . . He would appreciate the fight you have put up to save the Diamond Bar, Race."

Race shook his head. "He was right about me at the time," he responded slowly. "I've changed a lot, since." This was true. Fox would never know how much his original thoughtless liking for her had changed and deepened to responsibility.

"Oh, but father knew!" she caught him up. "He was trying you out in his own way—"

She was cut off by the rapid clatter of heels in the hallway. Spade McSween stumped in, his eyes blazing, his manner portentous.

"He's gone!" he burst out angrily, staring at Race. "I left him free to eat, and instead he dug his way out!"

Race was on his feet in a flash.

"Gone!" he echoed. "Madriaga?" And when Spade silently met his gaze he rushed on: "We've got to nail him, of course! He'll hit straight for Fontana's place! Call two or three of the boys, Spade, and catch up ponies! We're ridin'!"

# Chapter XXIV

## GONE TO IDAHO

The wild, lonely evening hour, with the wind booming over the desert flats, was a fit setting for the savage mood of Fent Crocker as he made his way across the range toward Nick Fontana's ranch.

Broad and blunt as his pugnacious face was, there was something hawk-like in the set of Crocker's head as he stared through the half-light. He had been alone for several hours, but he did not relax the fixed narrowing of his gimlet eyes; for he had just received the blow that he had never expected, and he was killing mad.

That afternoon, Angel Irosabel had come to him on the Lazy A and stripped him, without a tremor, of the weapon Fent had wielded against Race Cullyer—the cattle grazing permits without which the Diamond Bar must languish.

The interview with Irosabel had been stormy. Crocker had ranted his rage to the full. But old Angel was adamant. He had taken pleasure in telling Fent exactly why he must give up the grazing permits he did not absolutely need, and where they were going.

227

It had been the last straw—this defeat for Fent that meant Race Cullyer's triumph.

"He smashed me every way I've turned—made me throw away my money fer nothin'—made a laughin'-stock of me all over the range!" Fent gritted to himself. "But I'll get him! I'll ruin him as he ruined me—an' let him know I did it!"

The hatred in his heart for Race was tempestuous as he rode through the rising gale over a sea of wildly tossing sage. It was not lessened by the fact that he was powerless of himself and must go to the man he had once abominated, but who still had the wish to crush the Diamond Bar, and the means of doing it.

It was dark by the time the glowing window of Fontana's ranch came into view. Fent rode forward without haste or hesitation, a terrible certainty in his manner. Reaching the ranch, he turned his pony into a corral and then banged on the door.

No one answered for a moment, and Crocker pushed in without ceremony. The smoky lamp on the kitchen table flickered and all but went out. The wind snatched the door out of Fent's hand and banged it to. Fontana himself came through an inner door and stopped, staring at his unexpected visitor.

"What do you want?" he rasped, for the moment seeing in Crocker only another cattleman—another enemy.

In a tense, coldly furious voice, Fent told him the news he had received that afternoon—that grazing permits for two thousand steers were to be taken from him and turned over to the Diamond Bar. "I reckon you know what that means," he concluded harshly. "You're right back where you started with the Diamond Bar, Fontana!"

Nick was watching him closely. "So that's the price Angel paid for those sheep permits!" he responded, as though to himself. He nodded thoughtfully.

"The question is—what're you goin' to do about it?" Crocker demanded angrily.

Fontana was rolling a careful cigarette as he considered. His eye, as he glanced up, was keen. "Interested, eh?" he grunted.

"Sure, I'm interested! I know what this means to you, Fontana—an' I'm here to back you up!"

The stout Basque studied him absently for a moment.

"What makes you think I know what you're talking about?" he queried. The very mildness of the question was ominous.

Fent made a violent gesture. "Come off, Fontana! You know what Cullyer did to me, an' how I feel about it!" he bit out. "D'you think I don't know what happened to Luke Hamlin? An' that's just part of it! . . . I don't have to tell you

Cullyer's got to be smashed—or it means the Carson City pen for you!"

At Nick's arrested stare, Crocker went on swiftly: "Don't get me wrong! I don't know anything about them things—but I *am* after the same man you're after, if you've got a lick of sense left."

Fontana's deliberation was superb. "I'm 'after' no man, my friend," he denied flatly.

Fent's grin was wolfish. "I know you're not, yourself! You're too careful for that—and so am I. . . . But what about Madriaga, eh? Is he herdin' this spring?"

Nick took his meaning fully. "I don't know where he is," he disclaimed shortly. "Haven't seen him for several days."

Crocker's answering gaze was bitter with disgust. "Is that a fact?" he snapped. And at Fontana's hand-wave, he went on softly: "You fool! You precious fool! Have you stopped to consider that Race Cullyer may possibly have Madriaga somewhere on the Diamond Bar—hog-tied till he spills his story?"

Fontana threw down his cigarette. "You do a hell of a lot of supposing, Crocker! Maybe more than is good for you!" he jerked out, revealing the first rift in his armor.

Fent followed up his advantage shrewdly. "But then, if I should happen to be right?" he queried meaningfully.

Fontana thought for a long moment. He appeared to come to a decision. "Maybe we'd better talk business," he rumbled.

"We better *do* business—an' not waste time!" Crocker retorted, his tone exultant. Swiftly he altered the direction of his thought: "Where could you get hold of Madriaga in a hurry, Fontana—if he can be found at all?"

"*You* don't have to see him, do you?" Nick countered with inborn caution.

"No, but I'd like to be sure of what he's goin' to do," Fent came back strongly. "If we can fix it with him to—" He paused, listening to the bang of a broken shutter above the constant rattle of the windows.

Before he could go on, the door was flung open and a weird figure staggered in—Ramon Madriaga, haggard, emaciated, gasping, and badly scared.

"Nick! Nick!" he cried, and burst into a hectic gust of Spanish, his prominent eyes gleaming feverishly.

"Shut that door!" Fontana roared, trying to shield the guttering lamp with his body. And when the air in the room was still once more, he turned sharply: "Where in hell have you been, Ramon?"

"The Diamond Bar!" Madriaga ejaculated. "They keep me tied—starving—no water—for two, three days!"

Fontana clutched him with an iron grip. "What were they after?" he demanded fiercely.

Ramon flung into an impassioned narrative of his imprisonment. "I say nothing, Uncle Nick!" he cried. "I keep my eyes shut, even—I lay still—I wait!" His protestations were too vehement to convince.

"Well!" Fent Crocker interposed grimly. "Was I right, Fontana?"

The heavy Basque flung an admonishing, dagger-like glance at him. Fontana did not need to be told, along with Ramon's manner, that he was holding something back.

"Tell it!" he commanded imperiously. "They beat you—starved you—kept after you to tell what you know! And you told—what, Ramon?"

"No, *no!*" Madriaga jerked out without volition. "I don't tell—!" He clutched at his stomach, leaning against the table. And then when this abject appeal failed, under his uncle's remorseless stare, he faltered: "*Madre de Dios*! I tell about—the cowboy!"

"Win Flood!" Crocker inserted sharply, frowning. "That'll put Madriaga in the hoosegow, Fontana!"

"On with it!" Nick ordered the young Basque, his visage hard.

"That's—all!" Ramon bleated.

Fontana shook him severely. "Tell me!" he grated. "Did you blab about—Hamlin?"

"Ye-yes!" Ramon burst out, quaking.

Fontana was like a demon, suddenly transformed to fury. "Can they prove this?" he roared.

"I—I sign!" Ramon moaned.

"A confession!" Crocker ejaculated. "Hell!" He began to feel that he had come to the wrong place.

Nick had Madriaga by the collar now.

"Did you tell about me?" he bit out.

Ramon's eyes rolled in agony. Perspiration stood out on his brow. He could only nod, gasping, pleading hysterically all the while.

Fontana flung him down with a curse. Under Crocker's astonished eyes, the sheepman's arm jerked and his six-gun flashed and banged thunderously in the small room. Madriaga jerked, and then relaxed loosely.

"Are you crazy?" Fent demanded hotly, when he mastered himself. "This don't change a thing—killin' him! It makes it worse if anything! They got a signed confession!"

Fontana stared at him with an ugly expression, which slowly faded as a flash of sense came to him.

"No," he said disgustedly. "It don't change anything. This is a damned mess! How do I know what they made him sign?" He collected himself quickly. "But I'll beat the game yet! . . . I better clear out of here till this blows over. You better go too, Crocker!"

He began to move about, laying a rifle and a box of shells on the table, together with other things he would need for a quick flight.

Fent stared at him moodily. "I'll be damned if I'll go on the run!" he exploded at last. "They haven't got anything on me!"

Fontana was half-contemptuous. "No? Don't fool yourself! They can turn you up if they go about it! . . . I've been accused of burning the Diamond Bar hay, and a few things like that, but it'll never stick! And Crocker—it's no mystery to me about that shot at the Pinnacles that knocked over the Hamlin girl. Maybe it isn't to a few others! Stick around and they'll plaster something on you! They got just enough on you to give 'em the idea!"

Fent hesitated. "Well, maybe!" he grumbled. "It's bein' here right now that bothers me more'n anything!"

"You aren't so anxious for double harness with me as you were when you came, eh?" Nick goaded bitingly.

Crocker stiffened. "No, by God! I won't grab leather now!" he decided. "If you're goin' . . ."
He stopped, holding up a hand. On the wind was wafted from afar a faint clatter of hoofs. It brought them up with a jerk. "Somebody's comin'!" Fent snapped lowly. "Get that light out!"

Fontana knocked down his reaching hand. "They've seen that! Do you want to advertise yourself?" he retorted scathingly. "If you're comin' with me, leave things as they are, and dig!"

Ignoring Madriaga's prone form, they made for the back of the ranch house, and a moment later were at the corrals.

"That must be Cullyer's bunch!" Fontana muttered. "Ramon got away, and they trailed him!"

Half-a-mile behind them, up-wind, Race and three of the Diamond Bar buckaroos were closing in on the ranch house.

"Varian, you and Crebo ride around to the east," Race directed as they came to a pause. "Spade and I will go the other way. Nab anybody you see, but don't be reckless. I'll signal when to close in."

They separated, and Race and Spade made their way through the waving sage, their ponies restless.

"Maybe Madriaga ain't come yet," Spade suggested lowly. "That light in the winder don't look so queer."

"Fontana would see to it that it didn't," Race rejoined grimly. "Keep your gun handy, Spade. We may meet lead here."

They crept forward at a cautious pace now, watching with unceasing vigilance. It was not easy, for the clouds had lowered heavily, to seal the range in blind obscurity. There was only the dull glow of the light in Fontana's window, toward which they worked until Race drew in and dismounted.

"Not a soul around, outside," he murmured, "unless he's keeping a watch. That's what we've got to watch out for . . . I'll chance one of the windows, I guess."

"Lemme go with you," Spade urged. "Dang it all, Race—!"

"You hang onto my pony, and be ready!" Race rejoined evenly. "I won't take long."

He slipped away into the shadows, making his way nearer and nearer to the tumble-down ranch house, and keeping a keener eye on the dark corners than on the lighted window. He counted on the erratic banging of a shutter to cover his advance.

No one challenged him at the corner of the building. He sidled along the wall, six-gun in hand, and came at last to the window. Inside, the light made a halo around the kitchen table, but all else was in comparative obscurity. He saw no one. He was leaning forward to peer when suddenly a leg, extended upon the floor below the window, caught his eye. He stared.

The leg did not move. From its position he was sure its owner was unconscious, if not dead. His mind leaped at once to the reasonable conclusion—that he had arrived, not too soon, but too late.

Without ado, then, he burst in at the door. As he had expected the lonely place was deserted. The man on the floor proved to be Ramon Madriaga. Race swore and returned to the door to call the others in.

"Madriaga!" Spade exclaimed, when he viewed the herder's body. "Plugged plumb center! Fontana must've done this!"

"Yes—and Fontana's skipped out!" Race caught him up. "Our work won't be as simple as we thought!"

Baldy Crebo was kneeling beside Madriaga to examine him.

"He ain't dead!" he put in now. "Get some water, somebody."

It was found in a pail beside the stove, and a dipper-full was thrown into Madriaga's face. He sighed, weakly straightened his twisted limbs, and opened his eyes.

"Who did this, Madriaga?" Race demanded urgently. "Was it Fontana?"

The Basque assented.

"Where's he gone?" Race pushed on. "Was he alone?"

"I don't know—" Ramon whispered. "Crocker was—here with him." He shut his eyes again.

"Crocker!" repeated Spade, like an oath. "It don't surprise me none! They'll be high-tailin' fer Idaho, the two of 'em! Let's hit the leather!" He was all for starting after the two immediately.

"Wait up," Race thrust in coolly. "This fellow's got to be taken care of. One of you'll have to hitch up a wagon and get him in to town. Sheriff Denton's got to be told what's afoot too . . . Baldy—"

"Aw, Race!" Crebo protested loudly. "Blame it all, I don't want to . . . !"

"Somebody's got to go!" Race cut him off.

Baldy silently went outside and began to rout out Fontana's rattle-trap buckboard. As it turned out, however, he did not have to forego the pursuit of Fontana and Crocker. A herder materialized out of the night, scared and uncertain, who acceded to Race's demands. Madriaga was soon placed in the wagon and made ready to go, and the herder picked up the lines.

"Tell Denton that Fontana did this!" Race directed sternly. "We're going after him. . . . Come on, boys!" He turned to the buckaroos. "We'll hit north to save time, and pick up the trail in the morning!"

They swung into the saddles without further urging, and in another moment were pounding away from the deserted ranch, their faces hard and their manner intent.

# Chapter XXV

## "DON'T EVER COME BACK!"

Dawn found the Diamond Bar riders high on the Santa Rosa Forest Reserve. They had covered no great distance from Fontana's ranch during the night, for the rough trail had steadily risen; but they had the comfort of knowing that Crocker and the Basque could scarcely be expected to make better time.

The horses had been rested more than once. Race vetoed, however, any suggestion that they give themselves an hour or so.

"Fontana knows we're on his trail," he argued. "And he knows his weight will be against him in a chase like this. *He* won't lose any time restin'! Why should we?"

The others needed little persuasion, keeping to their steady pace. There had been little hesitancy in their course, even during the hours of darkness, for in that high country the cattle trails were the only promise of smooth going, and they knew the fugitives would not forsake them.

Ten minutes after the morning light strengthened sufficiently to read sign, Spade McSween found the trail they followed. He paused to examine it minutely.

"It's so fresh you can't tell exactly how old it is," was his verdict. "Certainly not more'n an hour—likely less."

It made them eager to push on.

"Hold in!" Race halted this leaping impulse firmly. "It's damned easy to wear a pony out in short order in this country! Crocker and Fontana may be lagging in the hope that we'll do it. And if we do, we're done!"

They acceded to his wisdom.

The sun did not rise this morning as was its usual wont, nor did the wind die down. The day was a gray twilight under lowering, fast-scudding clouds for an hour or more before it brightened gradually to an even tone. On the high ridges of the Reserve, where nothing stood between the rock masses and the frowning sky, the wind boomed with unbelievable force. The buckaroos leaned forward in their saddles, their eyes slitted against the invisible onslaught.

"We'll be out of the Reserve an' into the Calicos in another hour," Baldy Crebo averred, raising his voice in order to make himself heard.

"Yes—an' that means the goin'll be heavier yet," Stub Varian responded.

Spade did not hear this exchange, reading the sign ahead. Race paid no attention, his gaze searching the gaunt, rising slopes for the first glimpse of their quarry. It was not long before he was rewarded.

High on a rocky saddle on the flank of the Calico Mountains he caught the movement of men.

"There they are!" Varian seconded his discovery, while Race was trying to read some indication of the condition of the fugitive's horses. "We'll nail 'em yet!"

Crocker and Fontana crawled up the distant acclivity at a snail's pace, and disappeared through the bastioned gap.

"They seen us, too!" Crebo declared. "We'll have to watch out they don't double back or somethin'!"

All of them unconsciously quickened their pace somewhat. With the way plain before him, Spade gave over his tracking and went forward at a trot through the dips and flats along the trail.

They attacked the long climb to the saddle, the horses slowing to a plod. The climb seemed interminable.

"Wish this sky would break clear," Spade volunteered. "It don't make it any easier to see them two against the rocks."

No one answered him, each thinking privately that he would see the fugitives plainly enough for all practical purposes, despite the gloomy light from the clouds.

As they climbed higher, leaving even the lofty eminence of the Reserve behind, they experienced a sensation of vastness and space round about. The gaunt, gray-walled canyon chasms fell away below them, but they could see no great distance through the wisps of cloud whipping down the wind. The far Owyhee Desert was no more than a spacious void enfolded in gloom.

Long before they reached the rocky saddle, they were on foot and leading the blowing ponies to save them. The going was far from easy, with rugged slides to cross, and here and there a rock jumble to circle above.

When they were to the top and stood panting, it was to gaze over a field of incredibly broken stones, in blocks and fallen walls, dikes and jumbled, impassable mazes; directionless, without trails.

"Good Lord! They come to the wrong place, an' no mistake!" Baldy Crebo laughed harshly. "This'll slow 'em up aplenty!"

"Yes—an' it'll slow us up too!" Spade retorted quickly. "We ain't got a dally-rope on them birds yet!"

How much the difficult going had slowed Fent and Fontana was attested a few minutes later. The Diamond Bar men were crossing a comparatively open space amidst the rocks, when without warning something slapped a granite slab alongside of Race and whined away, to be followed immediately by the crack of a rifle from the rising slope across the rocky field.

"Jingoes! That was close enough!" Stub Varian sang out his own rifle at the ready, although nothing was to be seen. "They're beginnin' to get some worried!"

More slugs tore toward them, leaving gray smears on the rocks they struck. The crash of the rifles echoed through the lonely upland world. No one was seriously injured though Spade swore as a bullet ripped through his chaps, grazing his leg.

"It'll take more'n that to worry us!" he promised grimly, as they rode into the protection of upreared rocks. None of the pursuers had fired in return; nor did this cold firmness of purpose increase the confidence of the men ahead.

The buckaroos pressed on, exultant over the nearness of their quarry, and facing the task of crossing the rugged terrain without complaint, though every covert and ledge they met in their advance was fanged with potential death.

"Crocker's burned his bridges behind him now," Race told Spade when they drew together for a moment. "Not that he hasn't been near it all along—but that shootin' lets him in for the same thing Fontana will get!"

"He knowed the jig was up," Spade answered, "or he wouldn't have run with the bosco in the first place. There wasn't nothin' left for him, after you knocked the pins out from under him on that Lazy A scheme of his."

It was nearing noon by the time they won across the rock tangle and came out upon ground where tracks could be read once more. The trail of the pair ahead was plain.

"They're less'n half-an-hour ahead of us," Spade declared; "an' it don't look as though their hosses had any too much gumption!"

"I wouldn't say my own felt like a ball of fire right now," Baldy Crebo commented grimly. "But it'll travel faster'n theirs if I have to carry it!"

They forged on without let-up. It was Spade, riding in the rear for a moment, who called them back gruffly, at a point where the course of the fugitives had seemed plain.

"They didn't both go up this gully," Spade said shortly. "One of 'em turned up over the bank, here. See them scratches, an' that mussed gravel?" He pointed it out.

"Maybe they're worryin', kin they get through above," Crebo suggested fingering his rifle as he stared about the lonely spot.

Spade shook his head. "I don't think so. . . . What they're likely doin'," he went on after a moment, "is partin' company. They know it betters their chances if they can split us fellers up, an' pick us off!"

"What'll we do now, Race?" Stub demanded, impatient to be moving.

"We'll stay together, and ride down one

of them," Race decided without hesitation. "Fontana's the one I'd like to be surest of, but we can't tell which is which. I don't think either one will get clear away, though. . . . We'll push on after the one who went straight on up the gully, here. If I'm right, it gives an open ground above, and we can tell where we stand."

"Yes—an' if I don't miss my guess, that hombre is cornered on the bare shoulder of the mountain," Spade concurred. "I been studyin' the lay, an' I seen that some distance back. If he hadn't been starin' behind him so anxious, he'd have seen it too!"

They pressed forward without delay. The gully gave upon a bald summit, from which a long slope led away, curving so that they could not see far down it. They rode as rapidly as they could.

"There he goes!" Crebo ejaculated, as they rounded a rocky hump.

Race saw the fugitive at the same moment. It was Fent Crocker. He was flogging his horse down the slope, turning his face constantly to the rear. Now he began to fire his six-gun erratically, although the distance was too great for the lighter firearm to be effective.

"Never mind the shootin' 'til we draw up on him!" Spade admonished Stub Varian, when the latter raised his rifle, his face hard. "Crocker can't get half-a-mile before the slope gets too steep to do anything but roll down!—he's headin' fer that patch of rocks!" he added, as Fent changed his course slightly.

They pounded in pursuit unrelentingly, determined to cut down Crocker's lead before he found time to select his cover.

He did not fling out of the saddle at the rock pile, but kept on his six-gun silent at last. Gradually they drew up on him. Fent's terror was patent as he glanced behind. He brutally spurred his laboring mount.

Without warning the pony stumbled. It caught its balance in a moment, but not before Crocker, who had not expected the jolt, was thrown half out of the saddle. He brought up with a crash as his hold slipped, rolling over and over on the ground, and then scrambling up, gun in hand as he faced his enemies.

Automatically the Diamond Bar men spread out, anticipating the fusillade he would turn on them. Not a one of them but was more shocked than surprised, when Crocker flung down his gun hastily and lifted his hands, turning up an abject face. His hoarse, pleading cries whipped past on the wind.

"Well, I'll be damned!" Spade grated under his breath, his countenance ugly. "I shore never expected *him* to dog!"

Crocker was frightened white when they drew up their horses around him, guns ready to prevent treachery. He stared from face to face, chattering his pleas.

"Don't kill me!" he whined. "You haven't got a thing on me! I didn't do anything!"

Race stepped down and confronted him, his contempt for the other's cowardice plain.

"God knows nobody enjoys seeing you crawl, Crocker; but you don't have to lie to save your worthless hide!" he snapped. "You've done plenty, and I'll take my chance to wring it out of you! . . . Did you fire that shot at Pinnacles, or didn't you?"

"Ye—ye—" Crocker began. His fearful shuddering cut it off midway. His broad, coarse face was pasty.

Spade, on his horse, rumbled his rising anger.

"Did you burn the Diamond Bar hay?" Race flung at Fent, who shrank.

"Yes!" the latter confessed. The word seemed jerked out of him.

"And you tried your best to ruin the ranch—" Race was beginning, when Spade McSween let out a howl of rage.

"Lemme finish him right here, Race!" he begged. "Don't listen to him no more! Damn his rotten soul—!"

Race stepped between him and Crocker. "No!" he said inexorably. "Let me deal with this!" He turned back to Fent.

"Crocker, you're so black-hearted you don't

know what justice is!" he blazed. "You're so yellow you don't deserve to be called a man! I'm just as anxious to see you somewhere else as you are to go! . . . Will you get across the state line as fast as God'll let you, if we let you off?"

Crocker's terrified features flamed with a wild hope.

"Yes! Yes!" he almost shouted. "I'll get into Idaho, an' keep on goin'! . . . Don't let them shoot me in the back, Cullyer!"

The buckaroos exploded with gusty wrath, crowding around to get a clear view of Crocker, their eyes threatening.

"That's enough!" Race flung out. "Damn you, Crocker, I don't trust myself to deal with a skunk like you! Get on your horse and go, before I change my mind!"

Fent lost no time in complying, scrambling into the saddle with ludicrous haste and without reclaiming the gun he had flung down.

"And *don't you ever come back!*" Spade hurled after him menacingly, as Crocker made off at the best speed of which his worn mount was capable.

They watched him fade out of sight over a shoulder, and then with curling lips they turned the horses back over their own trail, maintaining an expressive silence.

"We've likely give Fontana a chance to skip!" Baldy Crebo broke it disgustedly at last. "And all fer that coyote!"

Race said nothing, giving his attention to the work before them.

An hour passed before they reached the point at which Fontana had turned off. They took his trail.

It was by no means an easy one, for the stout Basque had brought all his cunning into play, riding over bare rock and selecting what was far from the easiest ground.

"He's doubled back!" Spade declared, before they had gone far. "We must've passed close to him, a long while ago. Mebbe he was watchin' fer a chance to pot us!"

If this had been the case, Fontana had miscalculated. After a time, his trail diverged on its own course, although it still held back down the league-long slopes in the direction from which he had come.

"Nick's a wily cuss!" Spade admitted grudgingly. "He let Crocker lead us higher, while he was makin' time down the mountains! Wonder if he's hittin' fer the Quinn River Desert?"

They could not be sure. The trail led down and down, however, regardless of risky declivities over which their quarry's mount had slid on its haunches.

The afternoon waned with little difference in the state of the weather. The clouds were still lowering and sullen; the wind still keened over the gaunt and rocky shoulders.

"This here is tougher goin' than climbin' was," Baldy called back gruffly. "Fontana will soon bog down at this rate, unless he's ridin' a goat!"

They kept sternly on, all of them feeling the pinch of hunger, but tightening their belts and saying nothing.

"If he gets down where he can find a fresh horse, we're sunk!" Stub Varian burst out at last, giving expression to his mounting apprehensions.

No one answered him.

It must have been an hour later that they heard the eerie crash of rifles two or three miles ahead of them. Their eyes quickened, and they dug in their spurs without discussion. They rode on until they came out at a point from which they could see the creeping figures of men, drawing in a rough circle upon a high rocky butte, from the crown of which faint puffs of smoke shredded.

"Denton's posse!" Spade ejaculated. "They got Fontana cornered on that butte! The sher'ff is one bet the bosco overlooked when he doubled back. Race—you played a wise game, sendin' that herder to town with the news! Now Fontana's in a fix he won't wriggle out of!"

# Chapter XXVI

## THE DESERT DAWN

Picking their way down the rugged slope of the Calico Mountains to join the besiegers of the embattled fugitive Fontana, the Diamond Bar men were met by three of the sheriff's posse with ready guns, who were taking no chances on the newcomers. The sheriff himself was one of them. He stepped out from cover when he recognized Cullyer, and came forward with a keen face.

"Well, Denton!" Race greeted him. "I expect that's Fontana you've got holed up there on the butte?"

"It shore is," the lanky sheriff assented; "but why he's puttin' up such a fight against bein' taken fer shootin' a man who isn't dead yet, I don't know!"

"Fontana doesn't know that," Race countered quickly, stepping stiffly down to join the other. "How is Madriaga?"

"Wal, he's comin' along—was, anyway, when I seen him last. He'll pull through."

"You learned from him that Fontana had something to do with Luke Hamlin's murder, didn't you?" Race pressed on.

"Cullyer, that's a queer thing!" Denton

251

rejoined. "We gathered as much from the young feller's ravin'—an' that's why I'm here now with a posse—but when Madriaga come out of it, he was like a clam!"

"I expected that too," Race answered. "But it doesn't matter, for we've got a signed confession from him." He told Denton the story of all that had happened in the past twenty hours, while they moved up to join the line of men who were trying to capture the stout Basque.

Fontana was putting up a fierce defense. He had entrenched himself in a difficult position amongst the rocks, and kept up a discouraging fire. Several of the sheriff's half-a-dozen men had already been grazed by Nick's accurate sniping with the rifle, and one had been wounded in the leg.

Denton's men had spread around the butte and commenced a systematic raking of the rocks above.

"So that's how things stack up!" the sheriff ejaculated his astonishment, when he had heard Race to the end. "No wonder he's diggin' in an' puttin' up a real fight! But Cullyer, we'll smoke him out, or know why!"

They joined the attackers, creeping forward amongst the rocks which cluttered the slopes. The three Diamond Bar buckaroos had already dismounted and worked their way ahead, carrying their rifles, which shortly began to speak at intervals. The siege was continued with new vigor. Fontana must have been kept extremely busy, though he lost no opportunity for a shot at an exposed foot or an incautiously raised head.

Denton picked a torturous way up to within six-gun shot of the sheepman, and then raised a hand to such of his own men as could see him. The firing slackened.

"Fontana!" the sheriff bellowed. "You hear me?"

"Yes—I hear you!" Nick's contemptuous answer came back.

"Fontana, I'm callin' on you to give yourself up!" Denton went on. "You'll be safe with us— an' you'll get a fair trial! Don't be a fool, man!"

"Go to hell!"

Fontana did not trouble to shout. His defiance was iron, but his resigned voice dropped and went on in objurgations that could not clearly be made out. Further importunities had no effect on him.

"That settles it!" said Denton shortly. "We smoke him!"

The firing resumed. Men crawled from one rock to another, but their actions were hampered by the talus slope below the rocky crown of the butte—a wind-swept open space, sure death to whoever attempted it.

"This is a crime!" Spade McSween burst out

from a boulder near the ledge behind which Race and the sheriff had taken cover. "Ten of us fellers, an' no results! Denton, let's make a rush for that damn buzzard! We c'n git him!" His urgency was sharp.

"No!" Denton retorted flatly. "We'll git him, an' we won't throw away no lives doin' it, either! You jest hold yer hosses!"

Spade subsided, muttering. It seemed, however, that his rifle barked more savagely than ever, and at shorter intervals.

"Denton, we're about stumped," Race began at length. "Why not make a break for that patch of rocks up there to the left?" He pointed them out. "It cuts the range down considerable, and will give us a look into that crack across the butte. . . . Seems to me if the boys stir up Fontana from the west, we can make it okay."

Denton hesitated, but finally consented. He called Spade to carry his orders around to the west slope. Spade came crawling, listened noncommittally, and then started off.

"An' you be careful!" the sheriff admonished him sharply.

Spade grinned crookedly over his shoulder and slipped from sight. In ten minutes he had evidently accomplished his errand, for the firing from the other side of the butte increased materially.

"Now!" Race cried lowly.

He, Denton and a member of the latter's posse sprang up and began to sprint for the new cover.

Fontana had suspected a trick. His rifle began to spit. Race heard an angry buzz past his head, and Denton stumbled. Without thought of his danger, Race wheeled quick as a flash—to find the sheriff struggling to his feet, cursing.

"Keep goin'!" Denton bawled. "Don't let him git you!"

Race turned and ran once more for the rocks. A chip sprang from one of them, striking him on the cheek and cutting it, as he won to cover; the bullet whirred off into space.

Denton joined him, panting. The third man had flung himself behind a rock somewhat below them.

"Did he hit you?" Race demanded, turning.

"Naw!" Denton answered disgustedly. "Knocked my heel plumb off, an' like to throwed me a rod! . . . Let's git on up here an' take a look!"

They worked forward until nothing but the last line of low rocks stood between them and Fontana's stronghold. Here they were stuck. Peer as they would, they could see nothing; but Fontana tensely awaited any display of themselves.

Below Race and Denton, four or five rifles covered their position now with a steady crashing. For a brief moment these were silenced;

and at a scuffling behind them the two men rolled over hastily, staring. Spade McSween crawled forward, grinning wolfishly. Behind him came Baldy Crebo, nursing a bloody ear, his aspect savage.

"Let's rain him out with lead!" Spade suggested gruffly, pushing his rifle forward.

For once Denton did not demur. He raised a hand to those below, and at this signal, slugs began to rattle and scream off the rocky butte like hail.

Fontana's rifle was strangely silent.

For two minutes this state of affairs continued, before Spade swore gustily: "Hell! One of us nicked him—he's done! What say we dig up there an' finish it now, Denton?"

Race arrested him sternly. "Hold on, you hothead! That's likely a trick to get us to do just that!" He thrust Spade down without ceremony.

The latter glared at him blankly, and then exploded with weird curses. "How long is this goin' on?" he demanded heatedly. "That ain't the only game Fontana's playin'! Evenin'll be comin' on damn soon, now, an' then I s'pose you c'n git him easier'n he c'n git away!"

Spade's fears were well founded, as all of them knew. The cloudy, gray afternoon was drawing to a bleak close. Darkness would descend within another hour, and Fontana's chances of escape would be excellent. It looked as though he would get his chance too, for the besiegers were at a standstill unless some desperate sortie was to be made in short order.

"I'll just settle this in my own way!" Race said resolutely, at last. "I'm the man he's been after all along, and I'll take the chance alone! It's our only one!"

Before Denton or Spade could protest, Race arose and sprang over the protective barrier. His charge up the open slope was that of an incredibly reckless man. Immediately Fontana's rifle began to crash, uninterrupted by the attempted barrage of the posse. Race's hat went sailing. Dust puffed before and behind him.

"He'll be killed!" Baldy Crebo shouted hoarsely, unconsciously rising. He sank back when a wild slug spun him half around.

Miraculously, Race reached the lower barrier of the butte itself. To his amazement, then, and to that of all, Fontana suddenly revealed himself from the waist up, regardless of the danger to himself in the gush of his hatred of Race. His rifle was trained on the Diamond Bar foreman, and in his face was the killer's determination of a madman.

Race had no time to throw himself down. The hail of lead from the posse below had no apparent effect on the Basque. It was a moment as long as a lifetime, in which the swiftest movement seemed incredibly slow.

Race's six-gun came up at the same moment that Fontana's rifle flashed. The foreman had time only for one defensive snapshot, and to see the stout sheepman straighten and sway, the rifle rattling to the rocks, before darkness rose to engulf him and he sank unconscious, to slide a yard and bring up in a twisted heap.

Time is the all-powerful healer. Ten days after the fight at the butte, in which Fontana had met his richly-deserved death, Race Cullyer was on his feet and going about the business of the Diamond Bar with his old smile. Fox Hamlin had had him brought into the house and had nursed him back to health with a clean wound which healed rapidly.

Nick Fontana's ranch was in the hands of the executors. Rumor had it that Angel Irosabel would take a hand in its continuance. Ramon Madriaga was on the road to recovery, and was now under indictment for crimes which would land him in the penitentiary for life. The affairs of the range had closed over the disappearance of Fent Crocker and Blaney, the sheepman, without a ripple, and the outlook for amity between sheep and cattle factions was bright.

Hank Leflett had recovered from his injury received in Paradise, and was once more placed on the Diamond Bar payroll. Baldy Crebo's scratches had proven slight, if painful, and were already forgotten. Only Spade McSween was disgruntled. He saw life in terms of conflict, and the peace which hovered over Paradise Valley only whetted his dissatisfaction.

"Spade will never change," Race told Fox smilingly, when she asked him about it. "He was born breathing fire—but I will say for him that he never looks for trouble. It's his kind that have always helped save the plundered ranges of the West. We owe him much."

"But it is men like yourself who always give his kind direction, Race," Fox reminded, a light in her fine eyes as she regarded him. "Without you, he would be a force of destruction, rather than a defender of justice. . . . What is your secret?" she teased. "What binds you together—if you don't think I am jealous?"

Race flushed slightly. "It is more his odd idea of loyalty than anything," he answered reluctantly. "I once helped him stand off a bogus 'posse' that threatened to hang him for unexplained reasons, and he chose never to forget it."

"But the—posse?" Fox persisted, intrigued.

"It was a gang which terrorized the Idaho range," Race explained. "Spade and I helped break it up, in the end—another story. I'll tell you about it sometime."

Fox loved to tease him about these things, chiefly because it made him uncomfortable to talk about himself. But there were many other, and more intimate, things for them to discuss as the season opened. The tasks facing them would be hard; but they would no longer be rendered trebly difficult by the machinations of unscrupulous enemies.

"We simply must get our cattle on the range," Race said seriously one day in the patio. "I am well enough to go on a buying trip, and I must start."

Fox asked inquisitively about his plans, but he remained curiously abstracted, after this beginning, until finally gathering his courage, he turned to her frankly:

"Fox, there's no use denying that this will be a summer filled with long hours and hard work. We *must* repay Angel Irosabel, and start cutting down the mortgage. It can be done, and will be; but it will mean days and days when I am away— long silences . . ."

"Yes?" Fox prompted, with a quizzical expectancy.

"Why shouldn't we get married now?" he got out appealingly. "I couldn't be satisfied with anything else, and remain—as I have told you. And we could take a trip together to the Owyhee country, where I shall buy our steers, for a honeymoon. It is the best opportunity we will have for months. I—I have hoped we wouldn't have to wait, Fox. Can you—could you—?" He broke off, taking her by the arms and looking into her demure face.

She waited until he was done, and then smiled at his simplicity in love, lifting her glorious gaze to his without restraint.

"Did you think I would prefer not to?" she asked with gentle derision. "You foolish boy! I've been—only waiting for you to ask me, Race!" she assured him happily, as he drew her into his arms.

Only the purling of the brook through the center of the patio broke the silence.

Two days later he and Fox drove to Paradise and were married there. The buckaroos gave them an amusing charivari on their return to the ranch, joined even by Spade, who had been somewhat appeased by his appointment as straw-boss for the next ten days.

The lovers waited until morning before starting off on saddle horses, with a pack animal for the necessities of the trail, on their wedding trip to the Owyhee country.

June was drawing near. The desert was for the time-being green and aromatic with the bursting sage. The last vestige of snow had disappeared from the high peaks of the Calicos, hazy in the sun, and the clouds in the sky were fluffy white galleons sailing.

"It is glorious—all this!" Fox exclaimed, gesturing with a shapely hand, as they rode on into the afternoon. "People may call the desert harsh, but I love its space, its colors, its clean, strong health! . . . Do you remember the afternoon we went to Winnemucca, Race—and looked up the valley of the Humboldt at sunset?" She was associating the sentiment of that other hour with the happiness of this.

Race did remember. They rode on talking of that and of other things; for it seemed today that life was so full, and the future so promising, that they could never have their fill of the wonder of it.

The afternoon lengthened, the shadows ran out from the mountains like flags, and sunset came. They drank in its beauty with silent awe.

They camped beside a small creek in the eastern foothills of the Santa Rosas, and awoke to the cheery notes of a mocking bird skimming the sage. The air was cool and sparkling, the day fine.

Bacon was sizzling on the fire, and the coffee pot singing, when suddenly Fox rose to her feet.

"Look, Race—look!" she cried thrillingly.

The eastern sky was a blaze of gold. As Race joined her, the sun peeped out over the illimitable desert, touching the red earth and the harsh rocks with rosy life and putting fingers of light amongst the tumbled sage, while the shadows fled, fading.

"Dawn on the desert!" Fox breathed feelingly. "We shall never see its like anywhere else in the world!"

"It is *our* desert dawn, Fox!" Race told her happily, his arms stealing around her waist. "During the long night behind us, the shadows gathered to threaten us, and we wandered in darkness and lost the trail. But now the sun has come back again. It will be with us always, and the desert will no longer be our prison. It has become our home!"

The coffee pot boiled over then, and Fox sprang to its rescue. There was a light in her eyes that was more than the reflection of the sun as she and her bronzed, lean husband faced the problems of the new day, and those of all the days to come.

Books are produced in the United States using U.S.-based materials

Books are printed using a revolutionary new process called THINKtech™ that lowers energy usage by 70% and increases overall quality

Books are durable and flexible because of smythe-sewing

Paper is sourced using environmentally responsible foresting methods and the paper is acid-free

**Center Point Large Print**
600 Brooks Road / PO Box 1
Thorndike, ME 04986-0001 USA

**(207) 568-3717**

**US & Canada:**
**1 800 929-9108**
**www.centerpointlargeprint.com**